MW00353292

Push
Process

Jonathan
Walker

ORTAC PRESS

Text and images © Jonathan Walker 2024
All rights reserved.

The right of Jonathan Walker to be identified as the author of this work has been asserted by them in accordance with the Copyright, Designs and Patents Act 1988.

First published in Great Britain in 2024 by Ortac Press

ISBN: 9781838388782

A CIP record for this book is available from the British Library

Cover design by Pietro Garrone
Cover image © Jonathan Walker 2024

Set in Scala by Tetragon, London
Printed and bound in the Czech Republic by Finidr, 737 01 Český Těšín

ortacpress.com

For all the friends I made in Venice:
Alessandra, Alex, Anna, Cris, Filippo, Fritha, Gabriella,
Irene, James, Mike, Sophie – and especially Ulrik

Part
One

More speed, more light, more time.

But this is the fastest possible film, pushed as hard as it can be pushed; the lens wide open to catch every drop of brightness; the slow exposure shaking the image apart. Right up at the edge.

Go farther, closer.

1

RICHARD PICKED UP THE POLAROID SPECTRA CAMERA.
A chunky plastic body with a tight strap along the left side; a view-finder with a rubber eye cup at the back. A plastic lens at the front, next to a honeycomb sonar sensor for the autofocus.

It's not just the film, Merlo had said, a week back, when she was explaining how it worked. The whole thing's magic.

It *was* magic, he'd replied. When they invented it, thirty years ago.

But nobody's improved this – they bypassed it. Like old science fiction: an obsolete version of the future.

Can I borrow it?

Maybe it's been waiting there for you.

She was sitting cross-legged on her bed, a futon on the floor. She didn't move from there – only watched him stand up to take the camera from one of her shelves, where it was serving as an impro-vised bookend.

Now, in Richard's bedroom on the Lido, he released the latch to snap the camera body open. He pointed the lens at the wall in front of him and pressed the recessed button that triggered the exposure. *Pop* went the flash, bouncing back off the whitewashed surface to blind him for a second. The camera whirred and pushed out a wet grey print from a horizontal slot at the front. A protruding tongue, which hung down. Say *Aah*.

He sat down in the only chair in the room – a piece of moulded plastic garden furniture – in front of a makeshift table made from a sheet of glass balanced on two wooden trestles. He removed the slimy offering from the Spectra's ejection slot and placed it and the camera on the glass. In the dim light from the forty-watt bulb above, the sheet seemed to disappear, so the camera and print both looked like they were floating in mid-air.

Whenever you saw a Polaroid on TV, they flapped the print backwards and forwards as it developed, as if that was a necessary part of the spell. Superstition. Pressing the button meant letting go: losing control over everything else.

The print had a glued plastic coating surrounding the rectangular image window. A ready-made frame. Difficult to tear, or even burn – it shrivelled and twisted away from the flame of a cigarette lighter. The print itself was more fragile: if you angled it up to the light, you could see that the rollers in the ejection slot left tiny scratches on its surface.

The image took a couple of minutes to bring itself into being out of milky nothingness. This picture – of the wall in front of him – was empty, so it just turned from dead grey to white. The only things to mark it out as an image at all were a few spidery cracks in the plaster.

Richard's room was on the upper floor of a duplex apartment. The light bulb hung in a scorched vinyl shade over dirty wooden floorboards. Besides the garden chair and glass table, there was a camp bed with a metal frame, which had a sleeping bag laid out on top. A pile of phone directories served as a bedside table. He kept his clothes in his suitcase under the bed.

Not the worst place he'd ever stayed. He'd bought a small fan heater, but he wasn't going to be here long enough to bother adding anything else.

At least he had his own bathroom, next door. He'd just had a bath – if you could call it that, since the immersion heater only contained enough water to fill a third of the tub before running cold again. And it took an hour to manage that, so he usually washed in the evenings.

As he watched the print emerge, the door to his room swung inwards, and a silhouette he didn't recognise stood in the doorway, hands by its sides – as if this unidentified person had opened the door by telepathy. Mi spatchey, the silhouette said, with a terrible Italian accent. A man, who closed his eyes and pinched the bridge of his nose, as if he'd forgotten why he was there.

Di giù, Richard said. He pointed at the floor and repeated his instruction in English: Downstairs.

Laughter from the kitchen behind; Rage Against the Machine on a portable CD player. Richard shared the duplex with three German architecture students, who'd moved in here several months before him and had friends around every other evening. They had their own bathroom on the floor below.

All the buildings on the Lido were new – at least compared to Venice's historic centre on the other side of the lagoon. Richard's house was art deco on the outside. The ground floor was dark and empty, with iron bars over the windows – maybe the owner used it in summer. The duplex occupied the first and second floors – there was an external staircase up to its separate entrance. The inside of the flat had obviously been remodelled, and most of it was less spartan than Richard's room. A small landing separated him from the kitchen, which occupied a mezzanine overlooking an open living room with a high ceiling and a wall of windows that extended over both floors. Behind the living room on the floor below was a corridor with two bedrooms and the other bathroom. Richard's area was obviously an afterthought, but since he rented it separately and paid the landlord directly, including extra for his miserable bathroom, he didn't much like drunk guests trespassing.

He usually refused offers to eat with the Germans. As a teenager, he'd learned a basic truth: if you had to live with people you didn't know, you could make it more bearable by pretending they didn't exist. You could put up with anything, so long as there was a door you could close, to create a space that belonged to you alone. And even if you couldn't do that – he'd shared a bedroom for a year – then the inside of your head was a closed room.

Maybe that was why the Spectra fascinated him, because it was a closed room too, and everything happened in there at once: exposure, development and print. It reminded him of an anecdote about an automaton that played chess brilliantly. But it was a fake: there was a human player concealed inside. He imagined a homunculus inside the Spectra, pulling levers so the machine would do its bidding.

It was Thursday night, and the Germans were celebrating being more popular than Richard, again. Presumably they didn't have classes tomorrow. But since the state archive closed early on Friday afternoons, Richard wanted to get up early to maximise his time there. He was in Venice to do research for a PhD in history; his topic was spies and surveillance.

There were no curtains on his bedroom windows, so he normally undressed in the bathroom. But since there were people wandering about tonight, he put the chair under the handle on his bedroom door, turned the light off, and got ready for bed in the orange glow from the streetlight outside.

When he got into the sleeping bag, the chicken-wire mesh under the mattress creaked and groaned. It shifted as he moved, as if the mattress was a raft floating on the lagoon. He could hear someone doing a stage whisper outside his door in German, accompanied by giggling from the kitchen and, Sssh! (apparently an international sound effect). Then the door to his bathroom banged, followed by the sound of someone pissing, seemingly from a great height, faltering as the stream swayed off the water at the bottom of the bowl.

Richard had already taken a temazepam. He reached over to the pile of phone directories and rattled another pill out of the bottle there. Unclenched his jaw to get it in.

It used to be that the hours in bed before he fell asleep were his favourite time of the day, because it was only then he could be sure nobody was going to bother him. He played out elaborate fantasies in his head, a new episode each night – even if he could never quite remember where he'd left off the previous evening. But eventually he lost the habit of being able to fall asleep at will. And now the tension built in him every night as the evening wore on. It came up from his diaphragm, like the pressure in your chest when you tried to hold your breath. No difference between his heart trying to get out and the outside trying to get in. He clung to the world, or it clung to him – until he could find some way to loosen his grip.

He particularly hated being forced to listen to other people enjoying themselves: relaxing, laughing, probably touching each other. He imagined them standing around his bed – pointing, pinching him awake.

The temazepam revealed the truth: the noise in the kitchen was nothing to do with Richard. He'd chosen to remove himself from it, but that was exactly as it should be, because now he floated above it like God, bestowing his blessing on those who persecuted him. The world wasn't trying to get in. It respected his solitude: it buoyed him up. The thin mattress and the wire mesh became infinitely soft, attuned to and echoing his every movement. Not because they hated him – because they loved him.

Temazepam made him a better person.

When he left the house the following morning, he was the only one up. There were dirty dishes piled in the kitchen sink, and the Formica table was crowded with stained glasses and an upturned jam-jar lid full of cigarette butts. He leaned over the table and sniffed. He disapproved of illegal drugs, but everyone smoked pot here.

He drank a couple of glasses of water from the tap. Temazepam left a hangover, a dry mouth with a dull chemical residue, a grey veil between him and the world to match the winter drizzle outside. But even the hangover served its purpose – a different kind of insulation.

He took the 52 vaporetto to the Zattere. It was full with commuters at this time of the morning, so Richard couldn't get a seat, and the press of bodies moved him farther into the low covered cabin at the front. Out on the lagoon, the pilot accelerated into the tidal chop, so that the underside of the prow rose up out of the waves and bounced off the water's surface. The movement wasn't quite regular, so it was difficult to adjust to. Once, when the boat plunged into a trough, Richard grabbed the back of the nearest seat, accidentally touching someone's shoulder – but he was the one who flinched away. She turned around, but her gaze was placid, not accusing. Her mascara was running with the humidity. We're both dissolving, Richard thought.

From the Zattere, he walked up towards the archive, which was next to the Frari church. He wrote out a couple of file requests, then went to a bar next door and ate a brioche and drank a caffè latte while he was waiting for the documents to arrive. He was going through a file series called 'Riferte dei Confidenti': 'Informant Reports'. Letters and petitions addressed to the Venetian magistrates in charge of state security – and reports from men employed to watch foreign embassies and follow their staff around the city. He was focusing on the early seventeenth century.

The study room inside the archive had once been part of the friary attached to the church next door: the refectory, where the Franciscans ate together. It still had a hushed, communal feel, every sound echoing underneath the high roof. The archivist's station was in the centre of the room on a dais, from where they oversaw the entire space like an exam invigilator. The rest of the room had large tables, each with four numbered spaces where little red lights came on to tell you your file had arrived.

Richard had a basic laptop he'd borrowed from the university for this trip. As well as transcribing documents onto the computer, he wrote the routes described by their authors down in a notebook, and tried to trace them on his street map of Venice. The broad outlines of the city grid hadn't changed that much in the last four hundred years, and most of the street names were the same.

When the archive closed at two, he went around the corner to Ai Nomboli for lunch. The drizzle had stopped outside. If Richard photographed for the rest of the afternoon, and then bought a slice of pizza before he got the vaporetto back to the Lido, he wouldn't have to use the kitchen at home today. He loathed trying to cook at the same time as other people, bumping into each other, waiting to use the sink.

The sandwich menu at Ai Nomboli was displayed on wooden boards on the walls. The first few times Richard came here, he'd had to use a dictionary to figure out what was in what. Today he ordered a Miky, pronounced Mee-key: porchetta, smoked cheese, anchovies and sliced courgette. Porchetta was thin-sliced pork, but it didn't quite taste the way he expected – just like prosciutto was ham, but also not ham. While he was waiting for his sandwich to arrive, he took the Spectra out of his rucksack, and turned it over in his hands. In the closed position, it seemed self-contained, inert, like an egg.

The archive and Ai Nomboli were both near the main university building at Ca' Foscari, where Richard had gone to check the accommodation notices shortly after arriving in Venice. There was a whole wall of them there, in among obscene caricatures of graduating students. There was a graduation party going past now in the street outside Ai Nomboli, despite the cold: the laureata pelted with eggs and flour, a wreath hanging around her neck. The chant was already overfamiliar, after only a month here: Dottore, dottore, dottore del buso del cul! Vaffancul, vaffancul! *Doctor, doctor, doctor with an arsehole for a mouth! Up your arse, up your arse!* Grinning, capering friends. Parents and grandparents farther away, smiling awkwardly, pretending not to hear.

Richard drummed his fingers on the plastic shell of the Spectra. He had some notion of using photographs to document the itineraries he'd been reading about, and maybe, beyond that, to think about the *idea* of surveillance. He didn't know what that meant, but he knew he had no interest in the scene outside the window. He didn't go to his own graduation – either of them. What for? Fancy-dress parties.

Pretending to be a spy with a Polaroid camera wasn't the sort of thing the Cambridge Faculty of History approved of; nor, he imagined, did their equivalent in Venice, where even undergraduates did a dissertation based on archival research. But couldn't the present be 'like' the past, metaphorically? In a metaphor, 'is' was a way to articulate difference as well as similarity.

In the MA seminar on Theory and Practice last year, Richard had discovered the critic Walter Benjamin, whose aphorisms went off like the flash on the Spectra. *Not for nothing have Atget's photographs been likened to the scene of a crime. But is not every square inch of our cities the scene of a crime?*

Who was Atget? Richard went to the UL and found a book of his empty photographs of Paris from the early 1900s. Then in Venice, when he saw the camera in Merlo's bedroom, it reminded him of Benjamin's words. Didn't crime-scene photographers use Polaroids? It made sense, because the image couldn't be altered or manipulated. The print was discrete and self-contained. It stuck to the thing it represented. But it also peeled away as it passed through the camera rollers, like an encrusted bandage pulling away from a wound. And every square inch of Venice was certainly a crime scene, if you went back far enough.

He stepped outside Ai Nomboli. The singing had moved farther north, out of earshot, and the sun had come out. This was Richard's third expedition with the Spectra. Previously he'd tried to document locations in the most obvious, artless way: here's the Calle del Campanile, where Francesco Ongarin followed a visitor leaving the Spanish embassy in 1612; here's the Campo San Tomà, where the visitor went into a palazzo. But the images didn't have the pregnant vacancy of Atget's photographs of Paris. The light was flat; the plastic lens made everything cheap and toy-like. And the Polaroid process did something to the colours. They looked bleached, even when the print was still wet – as if it had been left too long in a shop window.

Try something different. Cut details out of the scene. Emphasise the rectangular flatness of the print within the frame. Make the picture *about* that. About the limitations of the process.

The modern fire station in the Calle Foscari didn't have anything to do with Richard's research in the archive – it wasn't there one hundred years ago, never mind four – but it fitted inside the frame better than an empty campo. Still fuzzy, but sharper than his other Polaroids. And not just because the subject was closer. Why was that? He looked up at the sun, then down at the wall. The light was at a tight angle to its flat surface, raking across it.

In the open space of a campo, light saturated everything, but in an alley – in *this* alley, right now – the sun's rays were focused into a narrow beam like a searchlight, and anything outside the sharp edge of that beam was in shadow.

Richard stood for thirty minutes in the Calle Foscari. He watched the sun move down the wall, then off it, onto the paving stones, then up the opposite side of the street. The entire city was a sundial, measuring out the day. And the sun didn't discriminate. It didn't only halo the palazzi and the gondolas, but Ai Nomboli and the fire station too.

This was what he had to do, not follow the invisible ghosts of seventeenth-century spies. They weren't going to show up in the frame, however many photographs he took. Follow the light.

He walked through San Polo, trying to find alleys the sun hadn't left yet – or where it hadn't arrived – until it was too low in the sky to touch anything except the tops of the bell towers. He moved the Spectra in closer and closer to the walls, scanning surfaces through the viewfinder until the autofocus warning beeped him back off.

It was a question of adapting the task to the tools you had available. He couldn't use Polaroids in service of an abstract idea. They were their own thing; they imposed their own logic. Did he want to follow that logic, wherever it led?

Maybe the right analogy wasn't photographer and spy, but photographer and historian. The city as an archive and the photograph as a document. In the Archivio di Stato, Richard had no say in whether a document existed or survived. Whereas with a camera, he went out and created his own.

Theory and practice.

POLAROIDS,
VARIOUS LOCATIONS

At first, it's only an urge. And it's enough to scratch the itch, for a while. But eventually you have to explain to yourself what you're doing. Establish some way of distinguishing between a good photo and a bad one – or even just one you like and one you don't.

In the nineteenth century, John Ruskin tried to create a catalogue of Venetian architectural forms. He surveyed the city and drew every possible variety of arch, pillar, capital. I seem to be doing something more basic: surveying the materials the city is made out of. Wood, brick, stone. Also: cement, concrete, plastic. The second group is just as 'Venetian' as the first. A decomposition of Ruskin's project.

Is that what I'm doing?

2

WHEN RICHARD FIRST ARRIVED IN VENICE, BEFORE HE MOVED in with the Germans, he stayed briefly in another flat on the Lido with a postgrad from Kenilworth University – a UK institution that ran a module on Venetian history in the city for a semester each year. Kenilworth rented the top floor of the Querini Stampalia palazzo for lectures and seminars, and kept a separate flat for the lecturers in one of the more modern parts of the city, somewhere off Via Garibaldi. The postgrad Richard stayed with, Stephen, helped run the course, but apparently didn't merit a room in the staff flat.

Before Richard left Cambridge, he printed out an email with instructions on how to get to the Lido: take the number 5 bus from the airport, then the 52 vaporetto from Piazzale Roma all the way around the outside of the city – or the 82, if he wanted to see the Grand Canal. But don't get the 1: the pisciacane – the pissing dog – which stopped everywhere and took forever.

He took the 82. Like most of the tourists, Richard stood in the open section of the vaporetto, in the middle – rucksack on his back, case on wheels gripped between his knees, squeezing himself into a corner behind the man in sunglasses who threw the ropes and shouted at everyone to move down inside.

On either side of the Grand Canal, the buildings were smeared and grey, and the water was opaque. Its surface looked like volcanic glass. People pointed cameras at the palazzi, and automatic flashes protested at the gloom. Even Richard knew that flash at this distance was pointless: today the city was out of reach, hiding itself, like a celebrity with her hand up in front of the lens. When they passed San Marco, all the people with cameras moved to that side of the boat, but Richard didn't want to leave his luggage. He'd never been abroad before – apart from a day trip to Calais at school.

He didn't have a mobile phone, but he'd bought a phonecard at the airport and he called Stephen from the bank of payphones at the vaporetto stop on the Lido. There were cars and buses beeping and zooming beyond the embarkation points. Careful: getting run over in Venice would be embarrassing.

He spotted Stephen from some distance away. No one would ever mistake him for an Italian. He was wearing a baggy army greatcoat over drainpipe black jeans and Dr Martens boots. An untidy mullet and aviator glasses. He was researching something on economic history – but it sounded interesting. Smuggling and the black economy.

Plenty of that now too, Stephen said.

Smuggling?

Working off the books. How the hotels and restaurants operate here.

Stephen didn't offer to help Richard with his luggage, but then, why should he? His flat had two bedrooms: a normal one with a double bed, which a mature undergrad was using, and another with bunk beds that Richard was going to share with Stephen until he found a place of his own. He'd have preferred sleeping on the couch, but that didn't seem to be on offer.

It only took Richard five days to find the room with the Germans, but he went out with Stephen a couple of times after he'd moved, and he met Merlo and Lars on one of those nights, when Stephen took him drinking around Campo Santa Margherita.

There aren't any bars on the Lido, Stephen explained on the way to the vaporetto that evening. Not in winter anyway. And the boats only go once an hour at night. So getting home's a problem.

Especially if you're drunk.

That's true even if you live in the city. Two of our undergrads have already fallen in canals. The staff have a betting pool each year on how long it'll be before the first one.

On the boat journey over, Richard listened to the whine of the vaporetto engine and the rush of the wake along the sides of the hull. He and Stephen were sitting at the back of the rear cabin, near the engine, so a faint hint of salt and rotting kelp was almost swallowed up by the diesel fumes.

The water's filthy as well, Stephen said. You have to get your stomach pumped.

Santa Margherita's near the archive, isn't it? Richard asked. Whenever he moved somewhere new, he tried to control his environment by scoring out familiar pathways, and only venturing beyond them when they were clearly marked in his mind. He hadn't got to Santa Margherita yet.

It's where the students go, Stephen said. But in Italy, that means anyone from nineteen to thirty, plus creepy Venetians trying to chat the girls up.

Do we drink wine? Richard asked. Most of his drinking so far had been from plastic water bottles filled with Pinot Grigio at the local enoteca, where the yellow liquid frothed as it spurted from the hose.

We're not going to that kind of bar, Stephen said.

What kind of bar are we going to?

One where you only go to drink – where they have beer. But it's more expensive than back home.

What should I drink then?

Well, I still drink beer. But the Italians have spritz.

Richard didn't mind these lectures – there was useful information in there. He could tell Stephen enjoyed instructing someone from Cambridge. There might even be an offer of friendship here: a recognition of a shared attitude towards the world. Everywhere's a shithole; here's no different. But that was a trap. If he accepted that common ground, he'd be admitting defeat, confining himself to being an outsider here. And he still had faith. Venice was going to be the magic place that unlocked the rest of the world for him – that changed him into an interesting and desirable person.

This attitude was easier to maintain after taking a temazepam at home. A cushion to stop Richard getting frustrated at the speed with which other people drank alcohol.

Stephen led them to a bar opposite Tonolo, the pastry and coffee shop where Richard sometimes went in the afternoons, which, he now discovered, was just north of Santa Margherita.

This is Cafe' Blue, Stephen said. There's others with colour names. Caffè Rosso, Café Noir, the Green Pub. We'll go somewhere else if any of our undergrads are here.

Why? I don't mind.

The mystique of command.

Richard peered through the condensation on the plate-glass windows into the bar's interior. It was gloomy inside, but there was an impression of a crowded mass. Whenever someone opened the door, it coughed out a fug of stale cigarette smoke, wet wool and spilled beer. There were people milling around the entrance, chatting and smoking outside despite the chill. The slick cobbles sparkled with reflected neon.

Richard followed Stephen inside, past an improvised mat of wet cardboard and a bin overflowing with splayed umbrellas. There was a coat stand by the door, bulging with jackets, but Richard kept his overcoat on. Stephen disappeared briefly around a corner past the bar to check the seating in the room beyond, but quickly returned.

Richard pointed. There's a couple of empty seats there.

I'd rather try somewhere else.

We're here now.

Richard moved towards the empty seats, squeezing himself past people's turned backs, not waiting to see if Stephen followed. Mi scusate, he said as he went, pleased with himself for remembering the plural form – though he wasn't entirely sure he'd got the sentence construction right. When he got to the table with the empty chairs, he pointed again, and asked the people already sitting there: Queste sono libere?

A woman with brown curly hair said, Prego, then turned away. But she placed her flattened palm on the seat next to her to stop Richard sitting there. On her other side there was a man with shoulder-length dirty-blond hair, who had a pint of lager in front of him. He didn't look at Richard at all – kept staring straight ahead.

Richard sat down and turned towards Stephen behind him. Va bene? he asked.

Stephen sat down and unzipped his coat. We don't need to go to the bar, he said. They'll come over – eventually.

Doesn't that cost more? Richard had read this in his guidebook.

Not here, no.

Richard tried to glance at the people sitting next to them without turning his head. The man was wearing a woolly jumper with a zig-zag pattern. The woman was wearing a floral-print dress over flared jeans, which were too long, so their ends were ragged and wet. There was a battered Pentax SLR camera on the table in front of her, with a bulky old-fashioned flash unit attached on top and a thick nylon neck strap.

Stephen was in his usual outfit. Richard was wearing a pin-stripe suit jacket he'd got from a charity shop. He liked to dress as smartly as he could. In Cambridge, he always ironed his shirts, even when he wore a jumper on top, but the Lido apartment didn't have an iron.

Another woman came over from the direction of the bathroom and took the seat next to Richard – the one her friend had saved for her. Surely Italian: rich black hair and a dark complexion. Tartan trousers with zips on the pockets and a blouse cut like a double-breasted suit jacket.

She turned to Richard and smiled. Chi siete? she said, leaning forwards to include Stephen in this question, and then looking back towards her friends as if they were being rude by not introducing her.

Non sono i nostri amici, the curly-haired woman said. She picked the olive on a cocktail stick out of the empty glass in front of her. A pause while she slid it into her mouth and manipulated it to remove the flesh with her teeth. She placed the stone in the ashtray on the table, then turned towards Richard. Ma possiamo parlare, se vogliono.

Richard ran his hands down the front of his shirt, trying to smooth out the creases. Sono Richard, he said. Riccardo. E quest'è Stephen.

The long-haired man on her other side took a cigarette from a packet on the table, but didn't light it. Why are you all talking in Italian? he said in almost accentless English. You're not Italian. We're not Italian.

Lucia is, the curly-haired woman said. And we're in Italy—

But I am studying English, Lucia said, taking a cigarette from the man's packet. So for me it is good practice.

You're lucky, the curly-haired woman said to Richard, English is the common language – even when there are no English or Americans.

We can speak Italian if you want, Richard said. Posso provare comunque.

It's fine, the curly-haired woman said. I'm Merlo. She pointed across the table. Lars.

Richard looked at them both. Are you from the same place?

I'm Danish, Lars said. She's Dutch. He pulled a lighter from his jeans and lit his cigarette, then leaned across Merlo to light Lucia's.

Is Merlo a Dutch name? Richard asked.

It's actually Italian.

Blackbird? Stephen said.

My parents came here for their honeymoon. I was conceived here.

Maybe in the toilet of this very bar! Lars said.

What are you talking about? Don't be gross.

I had to wait to get into the toilet at Paradiso the other night because two people were fucking.

It's not exactly romantic, the bathroom here, Stephen said.

Or the one at Paradiso, Lars said.

Fucking in bathrooms, Merlo said. It's even worse than sunbathing in San Marco.

Tourists, Stephen said.

That's not it. We're all tourists.

But you live here, Richard said.

Lars and I are studying art at Accademia.

So you're not Venetian, Stephen said. But you're not tourists either.

Well, who's Venetian? Merlo asked.

Stephen thought for a second. I'd say: anyone who speaks dialect, especially if it's their first language.

So, no immigrants then? I don't think it's helpful: tourists and 'real' Venetians. And everyone's so desperate not to be a tourist, to find the places where the 'real' Venetians go. I don't care; I go everywhere.

No you don't, Lars said.

Merlo ignored him. I'm a tourist sometimes; I'm Venetian sometimes.

But mostly you're a tourist.

We're guests here, Richard said.

What about the dishwashers and cleaners? Stephen said. Are they guests too?

Have you ever worked as a cleaner? Merlo asked him.

No. Have you?

A waitress. And behind the bar at the Irish pub for a year before I went to Accademia. Anyway, the point is not to be an asshole. I feel like I belong here – but there are different kinds of belonging. It's not a competition.

Venice has always been an international city, Lucia said.

The waitress finally arrived. Lars ordered a pint of lager, and Stephen the same, so Richard did too. Merlo asked for a spritz con Aperol; Lucia shook her head. The two women each had one empty glass in front of them. Lars had two empty pint glasses, along with a third he'd almost finished.

So you are both from England? Lucia asked when the waitress had left.

Yes, Stephen said.

London?

Stephen sighed and said, Birmingham.

Liverpool, Richard said. Originally. But not for a while. I've moved around.

Ah, Liverpool, Lucia said. I favolosi Beatles. Then tried to think of something to say about The Beatles. Richard made no attempt to help her. So tell me, she finally offered, do you think the Queen murdered Princess Diana?

Stephen blinked. Princess Diana? Why do you think we give a shit about her?

Richard had watched her funeral and cried, but there was no way he was admitting to that.

Don't be a dick, Merlo said to Stephen. It's a game. Like a party where everyone has to wear national dress.

I have a hat with horns, Lars said. I bought it here.

Richard tried to think of Dutch clichés. The first one that came into his head was the red-light district in Amsterdam, so he said, You live in a windmill then? He had a sudden, startling image of a dancing mouse with clogs and curly hair and a dismissive expression.

That's old-school. Normally I get pot.

The waitress came back with the drinks and a bowl of crisps. Richard went to take money out of his pocket.

You pay at the end, Merlo said. When you leave.

Don't people run off?

We're not savages.

Apart from me, Lars said. He slapped his knee and waved his cigarette in the air. Skol, skol, skol, skol.

Did you say you'd come here to study? Lucia said.

Richard hadn't said this – because no one had asked. To do research, he replied now, in the archive.

For a dottorato di ricerca, Stephen said. But I help run a course for English undergraduates as well.

Which university? Lucia said.

Kenilworth.

Everyone looked blank.

It's quite good, Richard said.

Do you go there as well? Lucia asked.

He's at Cambridge, Stephen said.

Is that good too?'

Stephen laughed. So they'd like to think. It's like Oxford. Old and rich.

They have English courses there, over the summer, Merlo said.

I'm not sure that's actually the university, Richard said. Is Venice a good place to study?

Accademia's separate from Ca' Foscari. But they're both good I think.

For some things, Lucia said. History, foreign languages.

What are you researching? Merlo asked Richard.

Spies, he said.

The black economy, Stephen said.

Isn't it difficult, in the archive? Lucia asked. I don't want to be rude – but your Italian's not *so* great.

Well, I've only just got here, Richard said. He pointed at Stephen. His is better.

It's not as difficult as you think, Stephen said. They're mainly legal documents, so it's a specialised vocabulary, but once you've got the hang of it, it doesn't vary much – like the sports pages in the newspaper.

How much of it is dialect? Lucia asked.

Witnesses in trials sometimes. But there's a 'high' Venetian for laws and so on.

Richard avoided documents in dialect whenever possible. There was only one copy of the nineteenth-century Venetian dictionary by Boerio in the archive, its pages shiny and translucent from the fingers of thousands of foreign historians.

I came here without any Italian, Merlo said. But I already knew English. And it's easier to learn an extra language when you already have one. English people don't bother. But you did. Why?

I didn't know any Italian when I started the PhD. I wanted to force myself to learn something new. Hold a gun to my own head.

All that, to be a historian. Merlo shook her head. A servant for the dead.

Didn't you come here for the art? Richard asked.

Yes, but I want to make something new. Pick the past up and put it to use, not stick it behind glass.

So what kind of art do you want to make?

I'm already making it, Merlo said. She took the camera from the table and placed it to her eye. She looked at him through the lens.

Everyone takes photographs, Stephen said.

Everyone takes the same photographs, Merlo said. You must show this, but you can't show that. You have to stand this way, and smile. Or: You can only photograph me when I've put on my disguise. When I've erased anything that might tell you who I am.

Stephen turned away from her.

You get used to it, Lucia said to him.

Looking away is a pose too, Merlo said. But poses can be real. It's clichés I don't like.

Richard kept his face frozen – tried to avoid smiling. He said, I can't imagine why you'd want a photo of us. What would you use it for?

I probably *won't* use it. I use almost none of the photographs I take.

This was surprising. But wasn't it the same in the archive? Richard transcribed page after page, but only the odd line here or there was ever going to make it into his thesis. You had to find the exemplary expression of an idea – even if the person writing it down had no idea they were communicating that idea.

He was used to people with cameras asking him to place himself in relation to them: Move back! Stand closer together! But Merlo moved herself instead. Small, precise adjustments. Leaning back in her chair, or forwards over the table, twisting her torso, tilting her neck and shoulders. She pulled her leg up and pressed her shoe against the edge of the table, then pushed back so the front two legs of her chair lifted off the floor.

Is your foot that interesting? Richard said.

It's a wide-angle lens.

The flash left a glowing blotch in his field of vision. Merlo flipped a lever on top of the camera body to advance the film.

Are you a photographer too? Richard asked Lars.

Me? No.

Lucia reached across Merlo to poke his arm. He's a sculptor.

He doesn't even believe in representation, Merlo said. It's all abstract. Like Henry Moore.

It depends what you mean by abstract, Lars said. I like nature – natural forms.

Stephen drained the last of his glass. I think I'm going back to the Lido, he said to Richard. I have to be at the Querini Stampalia early tomorrow.

I might stay, Richard said. He'd only had one drink. What was the point of coming here for that?

We're going home too, Merlo said.

Their home, Lucia said. I don't live there.

You should come with us, Merlo said, looking at Richard.

Do you have anything to drink?

I have grappa, Lars said.

Stephen said, I want to get the vaporetto before it changes over to the night timetable.

I'll take my chances, Richard said.

∎

After Stephen left, the rest of them walked to the bridge over the Grand Canal near the railway station. Richard went ahead with Merlo; Lucia and Lars were somewhere behind, arm-in-arm – she'd wrapped a knitted multi-coloured scarf around both their necks, tying them together. On top of the bridge, Richard and Merlo waited for them to catch up.

Why do you look at the ground when you walk? Merlo asked him.

Richard regarded his suede desert boots – a poor choice for Venice, since they kept getting wet. He said, I guess I'm trying to avoid stepping in dog shit. There's certainly a lot of it about.

Maybe that's the price you have to pay, if you want to see what's going on around you.

There's not much to see from here – only the train station.

Trains, in the middle of a city built on water. You don't think that's interesting?

Richard surveyed the Lista di Spagna and said, The Spanish embassy used to be on this street. Hence the name.

We live farther along, in Cannaregio. We share with an architecture student.

Snap! I mean, I do too.

When Lucia and Lars reached the foot of the bridge, Richard and Merlo moved down to street level on the other side and off up the Lista. Isn't this a tourist area? Richard said. There were still shops open, selling masks and ice cream and postcards.

It's all a tourist area. I thought we'd established that.

In the apartment, Merlo shushed the creaking front door and put a finger to her lips for Richard's benefit. The hall floor was uneven – most Venetian buildings had some subsidence – so Merlo's bedroom door creaked as well, and dragged against the floor when it was half-open. Inside her room, one wall was covered with bookshelves made from bricks and planks. Below them, a futon lay unrolled, made up neatly with sheets and a quilt. There were plants on the windowsill and an old-fashioned hi-fi underneath the sill, with a turntable and a tape deck. The speakers were up on the top book-shelf, with wires dangling down like vines. Opposite the bookshelves was a small desk with a chair on wheels. There was also a beanbag near the door.

You can take either, Merlo said, pointing at the chair and the beanbag. I'll get a couple more chairs from the kitchen.

Richard examined the bookshelves: a lot of photography and art books. An exhibition poster on the wall for someone called Nan Goldin. Another in Dutch for Ed van der Elsken.

Lucia and Lars stumbled through the front door, laughing – not making any attempt to be quiet. Lars slammed the bathroom door, while Lucia went through to Merlo in the kitchen. They returned holding a chair each.

Sit, Merlo said to Richard, waving him away from the bookshelves. I've got something I want to play you.

He sat in the chair by the desk.

Merlo slipped her shoes off without untying the laces and stood on the futon. She hummed a tune as she ran her finger over a sec-tion on one of the bookcases with a stack of cassettes, which all had handwritten labels on the spines.

What are you looking for? Lucia asked.

Alberto D'Amico, Merlo said. She slid the cassette out and opened the case. This is Venetian folk music, she said to Richard as she placed it into the deck on her hi-fi. 'Ariva i barbari': 'The Barbarians Are Coming'. From the 1970s. One of the waiters in Paradiso taped it for me.

A lone acoustic guitar and a voice – it could have been recorded at any point in the last fifty years. Richard said, I've never heard someone speak dialect. Cavaio? Is that – cavallo?

He's Venetian, Lucia said. So obviously the barbarians are on horses.

Or sunbathing in San Marco and fucking in bathrooms, Lars said, as he came through the door. He was carrying a bottle of grappa and four shot glasses, and wearing a plastic Viking helmet with horns. He put the glasses down on the desk.

'You ride like a Venetian' used to be a proverbial insult, Richard said.

Now it's 'You drive like a Venetian', Lucia said.

Can you translate the song? Merlo asked her.

It's about the founding of Venice, after the fall of the Roman Empire. Lucia stopped to listen and everyone else fell silent. So the singer's escaping from the mainland, and he hopes the lagoon will be a land of plenty where his nets are always full.

Pesse, Richard said. Pesce? Fish? The sounds are all flattened – like he doesn't want to move his mouth.

Lucia continued her summary. But there are pirates, and the biggest pirate is ... the doge! And now there's a war, to steal marble to build the city. The fisherman has to fight, and he has nothing to eat except beans.

So it's about the betrayal of the revolution, Richard said. Fuck's sake.

We didn't realise, Lars said, *we* were the barbarians all along.

Lucia flicked one of the horns on his helmet. Richard quoted Walter Benjamin, *Every document of civilisation is also a document of barbarism.*

Who wants grappa? Lars said, splashing the viscous fluid into one of the glasses.

I will.

Merlo shook her head. The fumes make my eyes water. Lucia tutted.

Lars handed Richard a full glass and flopped down into the beanbag. I always feel like this thing's eating me.

Lucia went to sit on his lap and they started kissing.

Do you know when the vaporettos go from the railway station? Richard asked Merlo.

You don't need to go all the way back to the station. The night one stops at San Marcuola. But you can stay here – if you want. She turned towards the multi-limbed creature on the beanbag. Can you do that quieter?

We'll go to my room, Lars said, disentangling himself, and pulling Lucia to her feet.

Merlo turned back to Richard. I mean stay in the lounge, on the sofa – I've got a blanket.

Richard knew he wouldn't sleep – he wasn't drunk or high enough, and he wouldn't be comfortable lying in his clothes under a blanket. So tomorrow would be a write-off at the archive. But maybe that didn't matter.

He looked over at the bookshelves. What's that? he said, pointing to a smooth plastic object at the end of one of the shelves.

That belonged to my dad. It's a Polaroid camera.

POLAROIDS,
VARIOUS LOCATIONS

Is not every square inch of our cities the scene of a crime? *What does a photographer look for at a crime scene? Clues, fingerprints. And who is the criminal here? Time. I'm looking for the fingerprints left by time on the city's corpse. They only become visible when a surface is dusted with light. And forensic analysis is not interested in perfect forms. On the contrary: it measures on the basis of deviation from a norm. It measures by decomposition.*

The photographer and the historian. What do they have in common? Time. They both make things out of time.

3

RICHARD WAS HAVING AN AFTERNOON COFFEE AT THE UNOFficial archive bar, the Caffè dei Frari, with Max, a visiting postgrad from the European Institute in Florence.

I wish I'd done that, Richard said.

I applied to Oxford as an undergrad, and they turned me down. So fuck 'em. They don't get a second chance.

Max blended in: he was wearing a powder-blue suit. When he sat down, he undid the jacket button and adjusted the trousers. He was drinking an espresso macchiato; Richard still insisted on a latte.

Richard asked, Do you have a limit to the number of times a day you ask the archivist for help?

Not really. Do you?

Twice, unless it's an emergency. Once in the morning, once in the afternoon. But I try to save up a few questions each time.

He checked the multi-volume Italian dictionary first. Then the Venetian one, for which there was sometimes a wait – or else you had to go searching for it on someone else's desk. But often the problem was that he couldn't be sure what the word was, because he couldn't make out the handwriting in the document. Or even if he was sure, the listed meanings didn't seem to apply. Sometimes he spent half an hour staring at the page, becoming more and more enraged, until he gave in and stood waiting for the archivist to look up from their desk and say Prego with a thin smile.

You need to make more Italian friends, Max said. The archive had many regulars, most of whom sat always in the same place. Max went out for coffee two or three times a day, with different people each time. Pity you're not a woman, he said. Then you could ask Alessandro for help as many times as you want.

I imagine there are disadvantages to that, though. What's he researching anyway?

Who knows? He'll never finish, so we'll never find out. Max took a sip of macchiato and rattled the little cup back in its saucer. How are the Polaroids going? he asked.

On sunny days these past few weeks, Richard had rushed out of the archive whenever he knew the light was about to hit an interesting alley within fast-walking distance. For any given wall, there was a short interval when conditions were optimal, although he didn't always get it right. He liked having something important to do, somewhere he needed to be. But it wasn't as interesting now as it had been at first.

I might have done all I want to with that, he said.

So you're coming back to us?

I don't know.

When the archive closed, he went to see Merlo, who was watering the plants on her windowsill when he arrived. She was using an empty Nutella jar, and some of the water dribbled over its lip onto the sill.

Watch the hi-fi, Richard said from the doorway of her room.

Merlo turned around, backlit by the window. Have you seen Lars's sculptures? she asked.

No.

I'll show you.

Won't he mind? Richard asked. Lars was out somewhere with Lucia.

I go in there all the time to borrow tapes and art books.

I don't know anyone else who still has tapes and vinyl.

Nothing against CDs. I just don't have a player here.

Lars's room was next to the kitchen, where Matteo, the architecture student, was sitting at the table. He was wearing an oversized white dressing gown with an *M* monogram on the chest pocket. Richard could see his bony ankles and red leather slippers under the table. He was eating pistachio nuts.

Ciao, Richard said. Matteo didn't reply; he shelled another nut instead. He had a bowlful on his left, and another bowl for the empty shells in front of him.

In Lars's room, Merlo closed the door behind them and said, Don't take it personally. He barely speaks to me.

Oh, I'm not in any position to judge someone for being anti-social.

Merlo laughed, and moved closer. She said in an exaggerated whisper, He always has a shower when he comes home.

Richard copied her tone. The dressing gown is special.

Lars thinks it's his way of coping with the bathroom.

The one here was tiny, with the toilet directly in front of a miniature sink, right next to the shower. As Lars put it: you can do everything at the same time, if you're in a hurry.

His room was no larger than Merlo's, but it seemed bigger because he didn't have a desk, and his bed was up in the air, on top of a wooden structure reached by a ladder, like the top part of a bunk bed.

Richard examined the construction. Nice, he said, but tricky when drunk.

Is that always your first thought? Merlo said.

He placed his hand on one of the supports and tried to wiggle it back and forth, as if he was testing it for safety purposes.

He built it himself, Merlo said. He used to be a carpenter.

That figures. He doesn't seem like a rich kid.

He didn't grow up one. But his stepdad owns a company.

Doesn't he get a grant? Richard wasn't sure how university funding worked in Denmark, but he assumed it was better than the UK.

It's difficult, Merlo said. He left school early.

So how did he get into Accademia?

Anyone can go to the first-year courses here. But then they fail a lot of people.

He's not in the first year.

He didn't fail. You have a different attitude, if you've worked first.

I have a scholarship, for my PhD, Richard said. But I was a night porter in a hotel. For a year before I went to university. Then another year after my Master's. It's not that big an age difference – but I feel older than the others.

How old are you?

Twenty-six.

She pinched his cheek. Aw, ickle-lickle, smooshy-wooshy.

How old are *you*?

Twenty-seven.

There were three bronze sculptures in Lars's room. Two squatting by themselves on the floor in the far corners, and one in the middle of the room, positioned at head height on a hand-made wooden plinth. Richard approached the plinth. Can I touch it? he asked.

Better not.

An abstract form, with curves and planes – attached to a marble base at both ends by foot-like outgrowths, and also via a thinner limb in the middle, but with gaps and holes you could see through. As Richard moved around it, the shape rippled and flowed.

It changes, he said, depending on the angle.

It's three-dimensional, yes. Congratulations on figuring out the definition of sculpture.

He looked through one of the openings and closed an eye to frame Merlo's face. Then shifted his position to blot her out – as if the statue was swallowing her. It's like an animal, he said. If you move, it moves.

You should tell Lars that. He'd be happy.

If you have a bust of a person, there's a front and a back. But here there's no face. Only a body. So it's always looking at you, wherever you stand.

Merlo knelt down to review Lars's collection of cassettes. She removed *Homogenic* by Björk and stood up. Do you want to see some of my work too? she said.

Yes please.

Matteo had gone from the kitchen. He'd wiped the table down, so there was no trace he'd even been there.

We won't see him again tonight, Merlo whispered to Richard.

In her room, she placed Lars's cassette in the hi-fi, then walked over to the bookshelf. I'm not showing you anything new, she said. I don't show anyone that – not until I've got it figured out. So this is from a while back. They're not even my photos.

Okay.

Merlo took down what seemed like a traditional photo album with an upholstered, cushioned cover and a ring binding. She carried it over to the desk and opened it: A4 pages, each with a smooth-down transparent cellophane cover sheet to keep the photos in place. She flipped past a few pages – each of which seemed to have a single print surrounded by torn scraps of paper covered in dense handwriting.

Richard stepped up to the desk, but made sure his arm didn't touch Merlo's. The prints were faded and old – the people in them wore clothes from the 1970s and 80s.

This is my dad, Merlo said. With his precious motorcycle. I used to be jealous of that thing.

Where is he now?

He died a few years ago.

I'm sorry.

Heart attack.

The photo showed a smiling, bare-chested man in jeans kneeling in a garage. The motorcycle by his side was stripped down, with pieces of the engine laid out on a sheet of newspaper on the floor. Richard leaned down to examine the scraps of paper surrounding the photo in the album. The writing was Dutch, so he asked, What does it say?

It describes two times I remember him hitting me.

Richard kept his eyes on the album. Neither he nor Merlo said anything for a few seconds.

Did he do that often? he asked.

Literally only twice – and those memories are so vivid, I'm sure I haven't forgotten any others. The first time was when he varnished the floor in the dining room and told me not to step on it. But I forgot and left a footprint, and he slapped me across the face. Then another time he left me outside a shop, and I thought I'd impress him by showing I could find my own way home. He went frantic – called the police. When he arrived back at the house and found me there, he slapped me again.

Why did he leave you outside the shop? You're not a dog.

I don't know. Maybe that was normal then?

My dad used to leave me outside the pub with a packet of crisps. But that was because children weren't allowed inside.

Anyway, I'm not saying any of this was traumatic. But obviously there are no photos of it happening. And that's what interests me. So in the text here, I describe his hands. In the photo, they're covered in oil. And he's touching the motorcycle with love.

Richard tapped the cellophane covering the photo. Your mother must have taken this?

Yes. But she gave everything to me a few years ago.

Has she seen what you've done with it?

God no.

Richard didn't want to talk about his childhood, so he listened to Björk yodel. Then he went to the doorway, where he'd left his backpack. He said, I brought the Polaroid back.

Bored already? Merlo sat down at her desk and flipped past a few more pages in the photo album, then closed it and brushed the cover, as if there was dust on it.

Richard took the Spectra out of his backpack. I'm not bored with it, he said, but I press a button and it all happens without me. I liked that, at first, but the problem is I can't make it do what I want.

Well, what do you want it to do?

I thought I'd discovered something, making everything *flat*. But it's only a trick. And the light. I liked that too, following it around the city – but now I feel as if the sun's telling me where to look. I remember watching you move with the Pentax in Cafe' Blue.

The world is a sculpture. It has three dimensions.

But the photograph doesn't.

So congratulations once again, Merlo said, for discovering perspective.

I never said I was quick.

You could try the Rolleiflex. Merlo went back to the shelves and moved a couple of books aside to reveal a rectangular black box with two circular lens openings, one directly above the other.

How many cameras do you have?

Only the three. The Pentax, the Spectra – and this. She took the Rolleiflex down and turned it over in her hands. It had several visible dials and levers, but all compact, packed in flush against the body. She passed it over to Richard and his hand immediately sank with the weight.

You could do someone a serious injury with this, he said.

It's not that heavy.

Compared to the Spectra.

It's the metal body. And it's completely manual. It doesn't even take batteries. It *ticks* when you press the shutter. But it's not exactly the future.

I'm a historian. I'm not interested in the future.

Merlo laughed.

I want to move on to the next thing, but I don't want to go forward. I want to go further back.

Well, the Rolleiflex is a classic. Ed van der Elsken used one for *Love on the Left Bank* in the 50s.

Was this your dad's too?

I think it was actually my granddad's. But my dad liked old things – he restored the motorcycle. So it's a way to connect to him. I mean, the bike's gone. But I can touch the things he touched.

The default thing is the natural thing, Richard said. I mean, photography's not natural, by definition – it's technology. But the default feels natural; you don't think about it. I *want* to think about it.

You should shoot black and white then, Merlo said. Because it's *not* natural. Not any more.

Are you sure you're not using this?

I'd rather it wasn't sitting there on a shelf.

Richard lifted the Rolleiflex up, as if he was looking it in the face. Why does it have two lenses?

Because you look through one while the other takes the picture. Here – I'll show you. Merlo held out her hands for the camera. The viewfinder's on top – she flipped it up – so you hold the camera at waist height.

Richard stood close to Merlo and looked down with her at the image of her room glowing on the camera's glass screen. It's back-to-front, she said, like a mirror. She moved the camera left and right so he could see the image shift, then said, The viewfinder is exactly the same size as the negative.

So the pictures are square?

It takes medium-format film. The best place to get it developed is Bianco e Nero. I'll introduce you to Vittorio – let him know you're my friend.

NEGATIVE 37/6:
RIALTO, 25S

Pick the past up and put it to use – *but not to make something new. To make something that's already old, even though it didn't exist a moment ago.*

The bridge at Rialto dates from the sixteenth century, but surely the steps and pavement have been resurfaced since then? Either way, they're worn from decades or centuries of feet. Electric lights at the summit since – maybe the 1920s? – but they must have been upgraded and rewired. The metal shutters, the canvas awnings – twenty years old? And they go up and down in a daily cycle. The Christmas lights have been here for two months. The commune leaves them up through January because they're going to be switched back on during Carnival, but in the meantime, they're dark.

Lots of people too. You just can't see them, because once the exposure goes over one second, objects in motion begin to erase themselves. Not erase; repress. Because they're not removed. They're shifted below the camera's threshold of attention, into the optical unconscious.

Different timescales: different kinds of presence.

4

RICHARD SPENT A MONTH STUDYING WITH THE ROLLEIFLEX —
every evening when he got back from the archive, and every afternoon or day when the archive was closed. He had some savings, so
he bought a Manfrotto tripod and a cable release, and shot roll after
roll of film, to get used to the viewfinder and the dials and levers.

He started with landmarks: for instance, the Salute church. He
thought of Lars's sculpture – the way it changed as you moved around
it. But he wasn't in a room – he was in a city. Now the church was
towering above him, and now it was far away, a tiny detail within
the frame. The scene wasn't inside his eye; he was inside the scene.

In Lars's room, there was no real relationship between the sculpture and the background – to see the sculpture properly, you had
to separate it from the background. But buildings weren't like that.
They were part of a larger context, so their relationship to the background – or the foreground – was part of their meaning.

There was a shop selling remaindered art books in Campo
Santa Margherita, and Richard bought one by the photographer
Gabriele Basilico, who treated cities like landscapes – he stepped
back and tried to take it all in. But in Venice, you couldn't step
back without falling into a canal. The few wider vantage points –
the bridges over the Grand Canal, the promenade alongside the
lagoon – were traps, because they funnelled your attention in the
same direction as everybody else's. It wasn't a question of being a
tourist or not – Richard needed to clear a space to stand, to empty
a moment out.

He decided to photograph at night, without flash. You needed a long exposure, but in one way it was easier. You weren't at the mercy of the sun, and moonlight was always weaker than street lighting, so you could go back to the same spot, night after night, and use the same settings. And since space in a photograph was distribution of light, night changed space. The city opened up; slowed down. And he needed to open himself up; slow himself down. Clarify the sequence; separate the individual decisions. Everything in slow motion, including the exposure.

Fog changed space too, but it wasn't thick tonight, just enough to soften the edges of things. Richard walked down each alley opposite the Salute, and everywhere he went the image on the viewfinder was too pretty. His first impulse was to fuck it up with a vaporetto. Even though it wouldn't show up on the negative directly in a long exposure, its navigation lights would slash the space in two: a Stanley knife across a Rembrandt.

He took a couple of shots like that, but he didn't trust the instinct. Vandalism: childish. Since he was there, he might as well get a clean frame. As it turned out, quite difficult to do that. Always difficult, to be simple. To stay clean.

Where was he standing? In a street leading to one of the traghetti stations: the public gondolas that went backwards and forwards between fixed points on the Grand Canal. The etymology of the word 'translate': to carry from one side to the other. In front of him, the moored gondolas bumped up against each other, like they were having a conversation. In the distance, he could hear the acqua alta sirens. The fog made everything slick and greasy.

He turned around in a circle, slowly. The Giglio vaporetto stop was behind him, so he photographed that too. Then he put the camera away, collapsed the tripod and started walking up towards Merlo's flat.

At the turnoff to Rialto, a small crowd under a streetlamp loomed out of the fog. They were playing three-card monte, the drama exaggerated – reversals, gasps, applause. Two obvious marks: Japanese tourists, smiling, still non-committal. Hard to imagine how anyone could fall for this, thousands of years after the game's invention, but Lars lost a month's allowance at the train station when he first got here, then wandered in a daze for hours, unable to believe how stupid he'd been.

North of Rialto the streets were as quiet as they ever got, and the fog diffused the sound of Richard's shoes against the pavement. Not a snappy report: an elongated scrape, decompressed. An echo, as if he was marching in time with himself, but not quite – half a step behind. The Coin department store, where he'd bought a leather coat after shivering through his first day here. He'd overestimated how warm it was going to be.

Out of the bottleneck, there were still some street vendors on the Strada Nova, in among the deserted market stalls. Senegalese with fake designer bags laid out on white sheets, ready to be scooped up in case the police arrived, though they were probably safe this time of night; Chinese selling electronic toys: crawling toy soldiers with stuttering, red-tipped machine guns; Bangladeshis moving from restaurant to restaurant with red roses. All men. Merlo said they lived in dormitories in Mestre. On the streets, the different groups didn't mingle with one another.

The Irish Pub was open, but Richard didn't need to piss that badly – toilets were always a problem, especially at night – so he turned off the Strada and headed north again, then left onto a broad pavement – the Fondamenta della Misericordia – which ran alongside a canal parallel to the Strada. This took him past Paradiso Perduto and towards Enzo's bar, where, even from a distance, he could see Lars standing outside, leaning on the serving window, smoking a cigarette and chatting to the owner inside.

Lars wasn't large, but he somehow seemed oversized: big eyes, big teeth, like the wolf in 'Little Red Riding Hood'. Tonight, he was wearing a duffel coat and a woolly hat with a pom-pom. As Richard entered the halo around the serving window, Lars said, Have you been photographing?

Yes, Richard said. And I've got some contact sheets from last week. He placed his backpack with the tripod on the floor by Lars and stepped inside Enzo's. Back in a minute.

The toilet at Enzo's didn't have a door as such, only a folding screen, and the hook to hold it closed was broken. Richard hitched his trousers up to stop the hems touching the floor, and whistled as loudly as he could. It smelled like Enzo had just thrown a bucket of bleach in here, and everything was wet: the floor, the walls, the ceiling. Droplets on the fluorescent light cover. The graffiti above the toilet said: *Michaela, ti amo sempre.*

On his way back out, Richard took a bottle of German wheat beer from the fridge. Outside, Lars had lined up a glass of draught lager for him, along with a packet of Pringles. Richard wiggled the bottle from the fridge at Enzo, who took it, removed the cap, then handed it back.

Ah sorry. Lars waved his cigarette, indicating the redundant glass of beer.

No worries. Richard picked up the glass and drained it with several extended swallows, then decanted half of the bottle into it. Problem solved.

Enzo worked here by himself most nights. His lower legs were swathed in bandages to stop the veins popping. Lars once saw him attempting to run after someone dodging a bill, and his shoes left bloody footprints along the Fondamenta.

You can keep Harry's Bar, Richard said. Like the Prada shop. 'If you have to ask the price, you can't afford it.' I don't need to ask. I *know* I can't afford it.

To Enzo's, Lars said, holding up his glass.

Richard clinked his dirty glass with Lars's. Where's Lucia? he asked.

Oh, somewhere.

Merlo?

She'll be along. She was finishing something in her room.

When Merlo arrived ten minutes later, she called out along the Fondamenta before she reached them. You're like *The Muppets*. The old men in the balcony. What are they called?

Statler and Waldorf, Richard said.

Lars frowned. The ones who are always complaining?

I prefer to think of myself as the Cookie Monster, Richard said.

Merlo leaned in and kissed him on each cheek.

Drink? he asked.

Tomato juice? she suggested.

Lars shook his head.

Cappuccino?

If you must, but it's sterilised milk.

Espresso then.

Enzo stirred himself behind the counter.

The street stinks here, Merlo said, holding her nose. Enzo's was next to a bridge that led back towards the Strada Nova. Past the bridge, the next section of the canal was blocked off and drained for dredging, but the work was behind schedule and it had been abandoned for weeks.

It's worse during the day, Lars said.

Let's go inside, Merlo said. She had her hands in the pockets of a cardigan, but she wasn't wearing a coat, and she was shivering.

The front room at Enzo's seemed bigger than it was because the walls were hung with a collection of mirrors. Richard looked at a picture of cartoon dogs playing poker: it was the only spot where his eyes didn't meet their own reflection. He, Merlo and Lars sat at a table in the corner next to a pile of tattered board games. Two students were playing backgammon at another table, but other than that the three of them were alone – it didn't get busy here until after midnight, when the other bars closed.

What have you got for us then? Merlo asked.

Richard took three eight-by-ten-inch contact sheets out of his backpack and placed them on the table. Each sheet laid out the twelve square images from a roll of medium-format film in strips of three, printed at the actual size of the negatives. It was a convenient way to review what you had before deciding what was worth enlarging and printing separately. Lars and Merlo took a sheet each, examined them, then swapped sheets. Richard stayed silent.

I mean, the Rialto one's good, Merlo said, but I prefer this. She moved her finger over to another image – of a vaporetto stop on the Riva degli Schiavoni.

Lars gave the other two sheets back to Richard and looked over Merlo's shoulder. Yes, he said.

Richard checked the two images she'd indicated. He thought for a moment. It's like tonight, he said. I took some of the Salute, and then I turned around – and the vaporetto stop was there. And no one's going to ooh and aah over that one. But it feels like a way forward.

And the Salute and Rialto aren't.

I thought about putting a vaporetto in with the gondolas, but why go halfway? Richard watched himself in the mirrors. Wherever he looked – there he was. He said to Merlo, I keep thinking of your photo album.

Oh?

The things people don't photograph. But what if you did photograph them?

NEGATIVE 37/9:
SAN ZACCARIA VAPORETTO STOP, 25S

Special privileges, special permissions, special access. Fuck that. I don't owe anybody anything. Anyone can stand where I stood, take the same photograph. It's all available. *And everyone uses vaporetto stops, but they're an embarrassment, the exact opposite of 'timeless', so no one photographs them.*

At night, the water reflects darkness. A black mirror. And since it's in motion, it erases itself on the negative, like people do in long exposures, but here the gesture's more emphatic, the effect's more systematic, because the movement's repetitive, relentless.

Show the movement of water indirectly, by describing its effects. Show the movement of people indirectly, by describing its boundaries.

5

THERE WASN'T MUCH IN RICHARD'S PIGEONHOLE WHEN HE came back to Cambridge in April: a belated Christmas card from his dad with a tenner inside; a long letter from his foster mum with news he didn't care about – he only returned to Liverpool now because his GP there prescribed without asking questions, and Richard didn't want to risk changing surgeries. There was also a postcard from Merlo, which she must have sent before he left Venice. The picture was a gaudy shot of Carnival maskers, primary colours like food-colouring dyes, but Merlo had scribbled over their heads with a biro. On the back, she'd written a funny story about Matteo in the apartment, and Lars had added a postscript. His writing was like a child's.

Richard knew his foster mum told people about Cambridge – but why had he come here? Perhaps just to prove he could. He'd got a First and won a couple of prizes at the end of his degree at Glasgow, and the lecturer who ran the course on Italian history said he should apply to do a doctorate at Oxbridge. But he now realised he'd arrived determined to hate the place, and hating it wasn't as much fun as he'd hoped. It felt trivial: a confession of personal inadequacy rather than a grand political statement. What did Merlo say? There were different kinds of belonging. Something could belong to you, or you could belong to it. But he didn't even belong to himself here. He was the ghost, not the people who'd been coming here for hundreds of years before him. He couldn't even see the place – there was nothing here he wanted to photograph.

The postgrad accommodation was outside the college grounds, in houses dotted around the city – like living on the Lido. Richard came in most days to eat at the buttery, and he liked to imagine the whole place collapsed into a sinkhole and replaced by a multi-storey car park, where he'd leap naked from bonnet to bonnet, setting off the car alarms.

He didn't drink in the college bar. Too visible. He went to nearby pubs – the Pickerel, the Eagle – but never the same place two nights in a row, and he never had more than three pints before moving on.

Returning so late in the academic year, Richard didn't have any say in where the college put him. He didn't care. He didn't even bother taking his boxes out from the storage area in the cellars under New Court. But there were a few books he needed, and he was glad he went down to get them, because he found something else among the cobwebs: the college darkroom. It looked like no one had used it for a while, so he brought his CD player down there, and he taped photocopies of images by Walker Evans and Berenice Abbott to the walls, where the paper warped and the ink ran. He got a book out from the UL on how to use a darkroom and taught himself.

The brick walls were painted white, but they were lurid under the safelight. Soggy boxes under the sink; ancient chemical stains on the concrete floor; pipes gurgling across the ceiling. Like being in a womb, or underwater. But here the liquids had a clean chemical smell: no blooming algae or kelp.

Richard turned the music up loud. The albums Merlo had played for him in Venice: Alberto D'Amico, Björk, *In a Bar, Under the Sea* by dEUS, *Rock Bottom* by Robert Wyatt. Under the music, he could still make out the sounds he needed to hear: in the dry section of the darkroom, clicks on the aperture ring on the enlarger lens, and the clunk of the circuit gates on the exposure timer opening and closing. In the wet section, the ventilation fans and the tick of the luminescent stopclock on the wall; the hiss of the open taps attached to the rubber hoses in the water baths.

He kept to regimented times in the trays. Two minutes in developer; thirty seconds in stop; two minutes fix. He didn't bother with latex gloves. He liked to be able to feel the changes on the surface of the paper, and the shifts in density and quality within the liquids. It was a point of principle to let the process mark you: Walker Evans had permanently black fingernails.

Today, he was trying one of his negatives from the Salute series. The church was out of focus in the background, and a fly-tipped fridge abandoned in the street on Giudecca filled most of the frame.

When he took the photograph, Richard had opened the fridge door, but it kept trying to close during the exposure, so he had to nudge it back open several times – you could see its ghostly creep in the image. When he first got the contact sheet back from Bianco e Nero, he'd been disappointed: the fridge appeared as blown white, like some ectoplasmic manifestation overloading the film with its power. But that was because the contact sheet applied the same exposure to every negative on the roll. When Richard adjusted the time and burned the left side of the image – giving more exposure to the fridge – he could separate the highlights.

When he took the exposed paper off the enlarger, it was stiff and slightly curled. He held it by one corner and slid it face-down into the developer tray, where it floated on the surface until he tapped the back with a knuckle to get it under – once at each of the corners and again in the centre, holding it down there. Then he lifted one corner of the plastic tray slightly, and moved it up and down so the tray twisted along its diagonal axis, creating a tidal back and forth. It took about thirty seconds for the thick paper to absorb the developer, and lose its stiffness to become slimy and supple.

A chemical photograph was the end result of a process, a recipe: a series of reactions, agitations and, finally, revelations.

At one minute fifty seconds, he lifted the print out with the same finger and thumb he used to place it in, and let the liquid run down off its surface, so that it pooled at the lower corner and dripped back into the tray. The lifting had to be done in one confident movement, otherwise the print would flop and buckle.

In the darkroom, the image revealed itself through sensory deprivation. A photograph exalted the senses it denied.

Next, he dropped the print in the stop: diluted acetic acid, the colour of piss the morning after a heavy night. This immediately changed the sensation of the paper, which now felt somehow dry, even though it was saturated. His fingers seemed to touch it directly, whereas before its oily surface repelled him. To push the print down into the stop, he switched to the fingertips and knuckles of his right hand. Left hand only touched developer; right hand only touched stop and fix.

He could only come to attachment through detachment. The way to intimacy was through the way of estrangement.

The fix rendered the emulsion on the paper inert, stopped it from continuing to darken when it was exposed to more light. It had the consistency of grappa. Even under the safelight, you could see its flow coalesce. And it stung when it touched broken skin.

He felt the power of emotion when he withheld it. Not repressed; not denied. Withheld.

Beyond the fix were two water trays, with a hypo-clear bath between.

This was his ninth or tenth attempt at the getting the fridge right – he'd been here all day, and he'd lost count. If he saved a version of a document on the computer in Word, it remembered all the changes he'd made. But here you had to start again with each print, and repeat the same adjustments, while the sequence got longer each time: expose, expose and dodge – which was the opposite of burning, withholding light to selectively brighten areas of the image – then burn, burn again over a smaller area, burn separately here.

He lifted the print out of the fix, and dropped it face-up in the first water bath, then turned the overhead light on. As if waiting for that signal, two people laughed outside. He could hear them shifting boxes next door in the storage cellar. He turned the music up louder.

Prints weren't really black and white: pure white was the paper base showing through, and like pure black, it was a dead, empty tone.

You didn't want much of it – only enough to calibrate the tonal scale. The fridge was pure white on the contact sheet from Bianco e Nero, but on Richard's prints it became different variations of light grey.

The 'now' of the photograph was there on Giudecca, squinting down into the viewfinder, then opening the shutter and waiting, waiting during the exposure; and there, in Bianco e Nero, with the developed negative glowing backlit on a lightbox; and here, with the negative projected on the enlarger; and here again, emerging with Richard in the developing tray.

Inside the frame, he cleared a space for something to appear, to reveal itself. To become a photograph.

At Glasgow, in his final year, a girl chose Richard to be her boyfriend. A new experience – why not? But he became restless and bored when they spent too long together. He assumed there was something wrong with him, but he didn't know if it could be fixed – or even if he wanted to fix it.

Early in his Master's year, he got together one drunken night with a French girl called Camille, and afterwards they'd orbited around each other for several weeks. He became obsessed with her. He didn't even know why. She was nice enough – she wore a college scarf and went punting. Maybe it was because it was the only real contact he'd had with another human being for months: like ducks imprinting on the first object they saw after hatching.

One night he found himself waiting across the street from her house, trying to spy her silhouette in the window, see if she had anyone else in there. She lived close to King's, and a porter surprised him – someone must have reported seeing him – so he put his head down and walked quickly away without responding to the man's questions. But Camille must have known it was him, because there was a letter from his personal tutor a few days later. Richard was scared of losing his scholarship, so he left her alone. But it felt like he'd chopped his hand off, and he couldn't get a tourniquet on it – except by drinking more.

There'd been a boyfriend back in Paris – a fiancé in fact – but Richard didn't care about him, or what he might mean to Camille, or even Camille herself in the end. When he tried to view the experience, it was pure white: he couldn't distinguish any detail.

At the end of the year, he scraped the merit he needed in the Master's. Camille had already left Cambridge, but he asked to take a year out before he progressed to the doctorate. He went back to Liverpool and worked in the same hotel where he'd been a night porter before leaving for Glasgow.

Perhaps he should have asked to transfer to a different university, but even deferring a year was difficult – he had to get a letter from his doctor. And it was part of his punishment to go back to the same place he hated and sentence himself to internal exile.

He pinned Merlo's postcard up on the wall next to the photocopies. She sent a new card every couple of weeks, and he put those up too. But he didn't allow himself to imagine her touching him. He killed the image with a drink or a tablet whenever it threatened to emerge.

There were no people in Richard's photos. Or rather, they were present in a different timescale, safe from his interference. *Almost* no people – because one blurred face refused to be ignored.

NEGATIVE 48/2:
SANTA MARIA MAGGIORE, INTERRUPTED AT 40S

Lousy composition, wonky horizon. What's the point?

It's a photograph of an event. The entire event, from start to finish. It's happening in front of the camera; it's happening inside the camera. The photograph's the event.

This is one of two operational prisons in Venice. I'm setting up the tripod on the steps of a bridge, so the legs all have to be at different lengths, and I can't get the alignment right. Amateur mistake, but it's part of the event.

All the fiddling about takes half an hour. Enough time for two guards up on the wall to notice me. They whistle to each other. I ignore them.

Two of them, but when they come down off the wall, only one steps in front of the camera. Stop now, *he says, in the middle of a two-minute exposure. So this is a photograph of the prison guard stopping me from taking a photograph.*

Acknowledge me; stop looking at me. How can I do both?

6

WHEN RICHARD WENT BACK TO VENICE IN SEPTEMBER, HE moved into a flat near the Arsenale with Max, who he'd stayed in touch with. Max was going to be in Venice for a year. His plan was to accommodate several different researchers in the spare room, each for a few months at a time. He said, That way I can be helpful.

The flat was on the ground floor, with a stainless-steel flood barrier fitted to the bottom section of the front doorway. You had to step over the barrier to get out. Max said, I live in suspense every acqua alta.

The house at the Lido had been a bourgeois fortress, set back from the street and surrounded by a low wall and a fence, but this flat was part of a neighbourhood. Even before he heard Max get up, Richard was awakened by the bells from the church at San Francesco della Vigna; then porters began moving things on trolleys past his window. Throughout the day, he could hear televisions and people talking in other apartments, cutlery clattering on plates; he could smell garlic and tomato paste bubbling on stoves, and detergent from the drying sheets hung between the apartment blocks. The only sound missing was the susurration of cars – in Glasgow he'd got used to it when he lived near the Clydeside Expressway. But that absence made everything else clearer.

Inside the flat, the rooms were filled with the owner's second-best knick-knacks in Murano glass. The spare room was really an alcove, set apart from the lounge by a curtain on a rail – another camp bed to sleep on, though less rusty than the one on the Lido. But Max usually retired to his own room early, which created the illusion of privacy, and Richard knew he was lucky to find somewhere cheap for a short lease. They even ate together sometimes.

The walk into the archive was longer now that Richard did the whole journey on foot, but he enjoyed the autumn sunshine. For the first few days, he went in with Max – at a certain point, they found themselves marching in step, and when Max noticed this he began humming 'The Imperial March' from *Star Wars*. But Richard was out drinking most nights, so he quickly gave up on nine o'clock starts. He decided to take advantage of the weather and split his time fifty-fifty between photographing and the archive.

He'd realised, in the darkroom in Cambridge, that he couldn't avoid it any longer; he couldn't photograph a city without photographing people. Theoretically, he could have used the Rolleiflex, but the waist-level viewfinder made him feel too far away. So with the last of his savings, he'd bought a 35mm rangefinder. New, but an old-fashioned design with manual settings. The viewfinder had a switch to flick between the approximate frame borders for different lenses. The body was a piece of shit: plastic sprocket, plastic film lever, plastic back. It popped apart if you looked at it the wrong way, and God forbid you ever dropped it. But the lenses were good. Richard bought three: a 50mm, a 35mm, and a 75mm; a normal, a moderate wide-angle, and a short telephoto. It was the first time he'd had any choice about how to frame a scene.

He didn't photograph his friends. He was still interested in history: the public and the private. The point where they mingled, like separate rivers emptying into the lagoon. So he rode the vaporettos. In Cambridge, he'd studied the photographs Walker Evans took on the New York subway in the early 1940s. Evans used a hidden camera and a remote cable down his sleeve, so he didn't frame or compose – he couldn't even use the viewfinder. He just photographed whoever happened to sit opposite him, like a CCTV camera. Anonymity: not only the subjects, but the photographer. Not self-expression – self-denial.

Richard could imagine what Merlo would make of that.

Evans claimed the images showed people when *the guard is down and the mask is off.* But they all looked the same to Richard, like mug-shots, because, even though the subjects didn't know they were being photographed, they were still trying to reduce their vulnerability to the gaze of strangers. There were no tell-tale gestures, no conversa-tions. No one was actively communicating with anyone else, least of all Evans. Everyone in the same null state.

Richard believed in composition, in placing figures within the frame, and placing himself in relation to them. He stood in the central section of the number 1 vaporetto as it crawled up and down the Grand Canal. Its overcrowded slowness was now its main attraction. The tourists clotted around Rialto and San Marco, but other passengers came and went according to different rhythms: old people, who had walking sticks and shopping trolleys, and sat inside the rear cabin next to the aisle, so you had to squeeze past them to get to the window seats; kids coming out of school, who descended like a chattering flock of birds and then all left one stop later on the other side of the Grand Canal. As the boat followed the twists and turns of the water, the sun moved from one side to the other, then back again. From Richard's circumscribed point of view, that movement was random – it picked out a face here and a hand there – but the randomness echoed the ebbs and flows of the passengers getting on and off.

He'd shot handheld before, with the Spectra, but he hadn't thought about what that meant. The Rolleiflex on a tripod remembered where you left it: you adjusted its field of view gradually, in minute increments. But on the vaporettos, with the 35mm rangefinder to his eye, the frame constantly emptied and refilled itself. He couldn't lock it even if he wanted to. His body, like the ones in front of him, was incapable of complete stillness. With the Rolleiflex, he was the camera's servant, and it was a lazy master. It did nothing for itself. But the rangefinder was an extension of him. He held it in his left hand, with the strap wrapped tight around his wrist. With his arm loose by his side, he could open his hand and relax all the muscles, and the camera still stayed in place, the front panel resting loosely against his fingertips and the lens hanging just below the palm, held by the tension in the twisted strap.

It was true: he took advantage of the omnipresence of cameras in Venice – of people's assumption that he was photographing the view behind them. But for Richard, the people were the view. He tried to cram them into the frame, like seeing how many marshmallows he could fit into his mouth at once. But he couldn't organise that many variables, so he ended up photographing them in ones and twos. It felt like an admission of failure.

The south side of Rialto, sun raking along the side of the boat as it headed in towards the San Silvestro stop. Like with the Polaroids nine months ago, the narrowing gap between the boat and the stop worked like a miniature alley to funnel the light.

Cut details out of a scene.

The prow of the vaporetto squashed into the tyres hanging off the stop; the stern swung around and cut off the funnelled sun, plunging Richard into shadow. The stop shivered and bounced back and forth, up and down, trapped between the bank and the side of the boat like a pinball bouncing between paddles – until the ropes tightened and strained and pulled the boat in flush.

At the last second, Richard stepped off the vaporetto. Moved himself to the zone of the stop between the exit ramp and the people waiting to get on behind the chain. Took off his coat and sat down; squashed himself up against the locked chest that held grit for the winter; bundled the coat up in his lap; changed the lens from wide-angle to the tighter 50mm. People laughed and pointed at him sitting on the floor, another crazy tourist. He didn't care. The light wouldn't be like this for long – the next vaporetto was due in ten minutes.

Even here, the hands weren't expressing a relation to each other so much as a shared orientation towards the approaching vaporetto stop. Runners waiting at the starting line for the pistol. It would be better if he could move around and through the crowd, while it moved around him. Not a confined space where he was cut off from the background – a *place*.

He began going to the parts of Venice he used to avoid, where it was most crowded: San Marco, the Bridge of Sighs. In the evenings, he met Merlo and Lars.

■

There was a new cinema in Venice at Santi Apostoli. Air-conditioned, two screens. The older places couldn't compete, so the cinema at Accademia was closing. In its final few weeks, it was showing some of its greatest hits from previous years: Merlo wanted to see *Before Sunrise*, but Lars vetoed that.

Why? she said.

It's *too* realistic. Like listening to people in the Irish Pub.

So they went to see *Wings of Desire* instead. On the way, Richard asked Merlo, Is it going to be dubbed?

I don't know. It depends what print's available.

The cinema was in a narrow alley opposite a nightclub. It didn't seem plausible there was a screen hidden behind the entrance doors and the ticket hall. After they'd bought their tickets, they had to pass through a set of curtains and two separate sets of swinging doors, which disgorged them halfway down a small auditorium, facing the gap between the front and the back blocks of seats.

The floor sloped down dramatically from the back of the room, and then up again towards the screen. The seats didn't seem to be level with each other, even within individual rows, like crooked teeth. The place was about half-full. Small groups sat or stood, talking to people on the row behind. Lucia shouted Ciao, ciao, then waved and blew kisses, seemingly to the room in general.

There were four seats in a row free near the front. When Richard sat down, the carpet felt squishy underfoot. Even here, he could smell the toilets at the back of the auditorium.

There were no trailers or adverts. The lights darkened abruptly and the screen crackled into life. Richard assumed everyone would shut up, but the volume of conversation in the auditorium didn't drop much, and people continued moving backwards and forwards between groups in the dark.

He whispered to Merlo, Is it always like this?

Yes, but I think it's worse.

Because it's closing?

Like gossiping at a funeral.

It was a poor print: crackles on the sound, and visible scratches and dust speckles on the image. It had the original soundtrack but added Italian subtitles. Since the film took place in Cold War–era Berlin, most of the dialogue was in German, but there were snippets in French and quite a lot in English. The English scenes involved the actor Peter Falk – Columbo from the TV series – who was playing a version of himself.

Richard didn't mind the subtitles – he watched the local programmes on television in the flat with subtitles too. Spoken Italian still sounded like a continuous stream to him. By the time he'd managed to slow it down in his head enough to pick out individual words, the flow had already moved on: like trying to photograph people in motion. But if he could *see* the words, he could follow easily. The collective face of the crowd separated out into recognisable individuals.

The film was about angels watching over Berlin, but since they were ghostly and invisible, they moved freely from one side of the Wall to the other. In the dark of the cinema, Richard took a plastic container out of his pocket and clicked the childproof lid for a ritual ten seconds before pushing it down and open. He glanced to check no one was watching him. Merlo and Lucia were staring up at the screen open-mouthed; Lars was checking messages on his mobile. Richard licked his fingertip and reached it inside the bottle until it stuck to a tablet, then brought the tablet to his mouth and swallowed. He wanted to float above the film like the angels over Berlin.

The print broke at one point and the loose end flapped through the projector. The cinema staff turned the lights up as they tried to splice it, and the chatter in the room grew even louder. Lucia passed a packet of mints along. The lights dropped again – whistles and cheers.

One of the angels fell in love with a circus trapeze artist; perhaps her fight against gravity touched him. If Richard understood correctly, Peter Falk was a fallen angel – not a demonic figure, just one who'd chosen to swap immortality for the pleasures of a carnal life. And the angel in love followed his example. Most of the film was in black and white, but when he descended to earth, it switched to colour.

As the tablet he'd taken kicked in, Richard thought of Hiroshi Sugimoto's photographs of cinemas. At the beginning of a movie, Sugimoto opened the shutter, then left it open for the entire running time, and only closed it when the credits finished. Blank, radiant screens: apparently emitting light, but actually reflecting it. Time incandescent and formless.

Richard imagined all his photographs as one photograph, a thickened present. An exposure of indefinite extension. He imagined taking more temazepam, one tablet after another, until he was swallowed by a tidal wave of indifference so vast it reached forward to his extinction, and back to encompass the moment before this moment, and out along a chain of similar moments back to his birth.

If he squinted, the screen above him almost seemed blank and radiant, like the ones Sugimoto photographed. Then it flooded with colour, and then the lights came up in the auditorium, and the colour came back there too – and here he was, in the middle of it all. He held his hand up in front of his face, and opened and closed it, as astonished as the angel in love drinking his first cup of coffee.

Behind him, seats banged against their backs as people stood, but Richard and his friends stayed still and silent.

Bellissimo, Lucia finally said. No one disagreed.

Are we going to go somewhere? Lars asked after another minute's silence.

Not the Fondamenta, Richard said. I have to get back to Castello.

Rialto?

Where? The fucking pub with the red phone box?

Let's go to Florian, Merlo said. It'll still be open.

Richard blew a raspberry.

It's not too expensive, if you sit al banco and order an espresso.

There's only three stools al banco, Lars said. We won't get them all, and even if we do, we can't monopolise them for an espresso.

A table then, Merlo said. My treat – so long as you don't order whisky or something. She turned to Richard. You have to go to Florian at least once.

They walked via Santo Stefano and along the street with the church with camels on the façade, past the guys selling paintings at the entrance to the Piazza. The café cast a rich yellow glow over the colonnade. Inside, the walls were gold and cream, divided into panels containing small paintings, everything shining under lacquer and glass; a softer tidal line of red plush rising up from the banquettes below.

I find all this kitsch, Lars said.

When they sat down at one of the tables, Richard said, When they made the film, Germany had been divided for fifty years – that was how things were, how things were always going to be. Then poof, two years after the film comes out – the Wall's gone. The people I stayed with on the Lido – they were all East Germans. They wouldn't have been able to come here before.

I think that's why Peter Falk's character was acting in a film about the Second World War, Merlo said. Because it's about history.

And the angels are historians.

Do you remember where you were, when the Wall came down? Lucia asked.

Our teacher taped the news and showed it in class, Merlo said.

Richard said, The photography was good, in the film. I don't necessarily mean the framing. The tones and the exposure: everything *glowed*. Like how Florian looks from the Piazza.

It was very romantic, Lucia said. Giving up immortality for love.

Merlo said, I've been secretly watching you in your trailer without you knowing, and listening to your thoughts – we've never spoken, but I *know* we're meant to be together.

Richard thought of himself, standing outside Camille's house in Cambridge, staring up at her window.

Merlo took her backpack off and patted it. She said, I brought another progetto to show you, if you like.

Yes.

Lucia moved from her chair over to the banquette, so she and Lars and Richard were all on the same side of the table, facing Merlo, who placed an A4 photo album in front of them.

I know these, Lars said. They're good. He leaned back to give Richard and Lucia more room.

Richard turned a few pages and said, I like how it's always in an album instead of an art portfolio. So, what am I seeing?

We should all be asking that question, Lars said, all the time. Lucia laughed at him.

They're crime-scene photos, Merlo said, but after the police have gone.

Yes! Richard said.

They all looked at him.

I just mean ... there's a quote by Walter Benjamin. How everywhere's a crime scene.

Well, I started by photographing one of those re-enactments, in Amsterdam. You know, where the police need information, so someone walks along the route where the victim was last seen, wearing clothes like her.

That's not in here, though, Richard said, flicking ahead.

No. Anyway, they don't happen often, re-enactments. So I researched all the murders in Amsterdam in the last thirty years, and I went to where the bodies were discovered. Of course, a lot were inside houses, because most women are killed by boyfriends and husbands.

So only women.

Yes. Anyway, for the ones in houses, I photographed the outside. Or the street, if I didn't know which house it was.

And those are the photos on the left-hand pages?

Yes. And I thought maybe I would find descriptions of what the victim was wearing, because you know how everyone's always obsessed with that – and then I'd try to find similar clothes, and photograph myself there. My own re-enactments.

Jesus.

But I had that reaction too. It felt wrong. So I tried to contact the families of the victims. And if they were willing to speak to me, I asked them how they wanted their daughter or sister to be remembered. And I went to their houses and I photographed them holding their favourite photo of her. And afterwards I wrote down a story they told me. So that's the idea. The crime scene, the family. They're both about what's missing – and it's the same person *not* there in each – but the absence has a different shape.

Objective and subjective, Lars said.

Except I don't believe in objectivity.

Most of the photos were shot with flash. Since the crime-scene images had been taken at night, this meant the foreground was brilliantly lit, and the background disappeared completely – but there was nothing in the foreground either. Just gravel, or tarmac, or weeds. The interiors on the opposite page were crowded with furniture, but they felt just as haunted. The backgrounds weren't as dark as the exterior shots, because the walls of the rooms were closer to the camera, and they caught the flash, but the people sitting in armchairs or huddled on sofas looked like they were the ones lying on a morgue table under God's spotlight. Sometimes you couldn't even see the photos they held, because the glass over the framed prints reflected the flash too.

What do you think? Merlo asked.

Richard made his way through several pages, slowing himself down so he stayed on each spread for several seconds, like he was walking over the landscape, or sitting in the room with the bereaved family, listening. Then he tapped the book towards Lucia, who'd been watching over his shoulder.

I think, he finally said to Merlo, that you're a better photographer than me.

She shrugged.

That's not the problem. The problem is: you're also a better historian.

You need to get up close – you can't look down from on high.

A waiter in a white jacket arrived with their drinks. He flourished them on a silver tray, and placed them on the table with exaggerated movements. Merlo moved her album out of his way. Teapots and porcelain cups: Twinings for Merlo; camomile for Lucia; hot chocolate for Richard. Lars refused to drink anything here on principle. Before he left, the waiter made a little bow and said, Prego, even though no one had spoken to him. Lucia said, Grazie, but he was already walking away.

I hate the waiters here, Lars said. They think they're better than you.

Richard watched his friends move their hands around the cups. Lars had small cuts from the chisel, and older scars; white dust around his fingernails. Merlo bit her nails savagely, so she looked like she'd escaped from a Gestapo prison – she wore a thin, tarnished silver ring. Lucia's nails were immaculate: she wasn't wearing coloured varnish, but she'd painted them with transparent lacquer, and she wore a couple of chunky rings, one with a garnet.

Richard said, I brought something too. Just contacts. They're 35mm, so I have a loupe.

The café was nearly empty, so Merlo said, Put them on the next table. They won't mind.

Are you sure about that? Lars said.

Richard did as Merlo suggested, and the four of them gathered around the second table but remained standing, as if to imply they'd only borrowed it for a moment. Merlo and Lars took it in turns to lean over and move the loupe along the surface of the eight-by-ten sheets.

Why are they all in the daytime? Merlo said. I thought you wanted to work at night.

I don't want to use flash, Richard said. And I can't use a tripod for this type of picture.

You could push process, Merlo said.

I *could*.

What does that mean? Lucia asked.

You take a 3200 film, Merlo said, which is really 1600 by the way, so you're already pushing it at 3200. Then you expose it *as if* it's faster.

In other words, you deliberately underexpose, Richard said.

And then you overdevelop to compensate.

And that works? Lucia said.

Well, it's grainy as fuck to begin with, Merlo said, and pushing makes it worse. Plus you lose shadow detail, and the highlights blow.

In other words, it's shit, Richard said.

But it means you can work handheld at night.

Barely.

Stop trying to be perfect.

Get your hands dirty, Lars said.

Fall in love, Lucia said.

Richard said, I didn't like how black and white was a disability, in the film – a lack. It's not like that. You take something away, because it makes things clearer, purer. You can see it better.

But you're not an angel, Merlo said. You have a point of view because you have a body, because you're *visible*. She reached across the table and held his face between her hands. You can only see me because I can see you.

NEGATIVE 106/10:
PALAZZO DUCALE, 1/125S

One way of defining public space, communal space, is the absence of the right to privacy. So if you fall asleep in one of the most photographed places in the world, tough luck, you're fair game, even if in your own mind you're a self-constituted republic of two, marking off your own little boudoir. You're part of a larger scene, whether you like it or not.

What is the larger scene? Take a step back; change to a wider lens.

There are always parts of communal areas cordoned off for repairs, and that's why the wire fence is there in the background. It defines public space by removing bits of it. And Venice has narrow wooden pathways, which are laid out on metal supports, to keep your feet dry in floods. So walking on water is a collective miracle, performed at regular intervals. But no floods today, so the boards are stacked out of the way. That's what the lovers are sleeping on.

There's a political rally somewhere nearby: the guys with rosettes on the right. The woman coming in from the opposite side is probably Venetian too, because she couldn't give a shit. Indifference is how Venetians distinguish themselves from tourists – like the pair in the background, the only people looking at me.

Everyone's falling away from each other in the frame, but the lovers keep a tight grip. A fixed point, around which the world turns.

I could keep going, shot after shot, but there's a limit. Don't push it; don't try and remake a moment that's gone. Maybe I got it, maybe I didn't.

7

RICHARD CLOSED HIS RIGHT EYE AND PLACED HIS INDEX finger against the lid. As his left eye scanned the room, there was a corresponding movement in the blind eye under his fingertip. Saccades: that was the word. It drew attention to itself in a sentence, like a dramatic gesture in a frame, but it described a different kind of looking, which didn't prioritise dramatic gestures.

With a crowd, he'd discovered the best approach was to defocus, generalise his attention. To almost withdraw, as if he was distracted, glazing over, as if he wasn't an I. Or rather, not at the centre of his I. A glance, not a stare. But shooting at night was different, because he was working against the limits of the film and the camera. He had to make a choice, because with the lens wide open, the depth of field was non-existent and the focal plane was a guillotine cutting across the scene. Where was the energy in the room?

Are you winking at me? Merlo asked.

I've got something in my eye.

What?

You, he thought. You're in my eye.

He normally didn't bring his camera when he was out with her, because he was too shy to let her see him working – and because, like tonight, she often had her Pentax, and he didn't want to compete. He'd brought the rangefinder tonight, but it was a mistake, because every time he pulled it up towards his eye, she moved with the Pentax too. When he finally gave in and swung the rangefinder in her direction, she popped her flash at the same moment he pressed the shutter release.

Got you, she said.

Behind her, a dark room filled with muttering tables. What was he missing? Nothing. No individuation of a face, no defined movement of a body. No energy, which only meant he wasn't bringing any energy to it.

They were in Paradiso Perduto with Max, waiting for Lars and Lucia – and Max's friend Tommaso. Merlo was wearing a hoodie over some hideous tie-dye leggings, because nowhere on the Fondamenta counted as going out. Max was in a short burgundy leather jacket with an elasticated cotton waist and cuffs, and a tweed cap with a popper on the peak.

There was a band playing at Paradiso tonight, local jazz fans doing their best. The piano belonged to the bar – Richard suspected it wasn't fully in tune – but it was joined tonight by a trumpet, double bass and drums. Richard and his friends were beyond the musicians, in the main section of the interior, which had three long rows of tables.

These were laid out in unbroken lines, all the way to the kitchen at the back of the room, and each row had benches on both sides – like a refectory.

On the other side of the musicians, just inside the doors onto the Fondamenta, there was an open space and a serving area: a bar with beer taps and a separate section behind glass for cicchetti with portions of squid and mussels. There was a moth-eaten rocking horse by the windows, and people piled their coats over its saddle.

Have you been to the casino? Merlo asked Max. They'd been discussing his research on the history of gambling in Venice.

Once. But watching is boring. There has to be something at stake for you personally, or it ruins the illusion, and suddenly all you can see are the mouldy curtains, the middle-aged playboys with yellow stains on their fingertips. He turned to Richard and pointed at the rangefinder. Why don't you use a flash?

Because I don't like to add anything.

Because he photographs strangers and he doesn't want to get punched in the face, Merlo said.

Does it come out? Max said.

Not usually, no, Richard said.

Photography was a gambling game too. Merlo had taught him that. Each exposure was an attempt to define the difference between winning and losing – an arbitrary and absolute distinction, which only mattered because the players decided to agree it did. The machine registered every scene with equal indifference, just as the roulette wheel didn't care where the ball landed. But in this game the uncontrollable element lay in not being able to define a winning move in advance. You had to figure out later if and why you'd won.

An Italian in a V-neck sweater touched Max on the shoulder and placed two fingers against his own lips. Max nudged his cigarette packet across the table. The Italian's fingers spidered their way between the empty glasses.

I still can't get over that, Richard said when he'd gone. Bumming cigarettes. Shameless.

Everybody does it, Merlo said. They're cheaper here.

I don't get why you'd ask a stranger for anything.

I never buy cigarettes, Merlo said. That's how I limit the number I smoke. Only the ones I can get for free.

Nooo, Max said, reeling back. You're abusing the system.

Lars and Lucia were making their way through the crowd around the entrance, where the jazz boys were having a well-earned drink, and she clapped her hands when she got close. Max!

Hey, Lars said, not looking at anyone in particular.

Max touched the peak of his cap as if he was about to stand up and take it off. Lucia sat down next to him and threaded her arm through his. Lars flopped down onto the bench on her other side and burped. Lucia smacked him on the back of the head.

Have we missed the music? he said.

Yes, Max said.

Good.

Don't be mean, Richard said.

I'm only joking. I always come here when they're playing.

Where were you tonight then?

Well, Lars said, and Lucia blushed.

Che volete? Max asked, including the whole group in the gesture.

The mulled wine is nice, Merlo said to Lucia.

I'll have a red beer, Richard said.

Blonde for me, Lars said.

I will help you, Lucia said to Max, standing with him and shrugging off her sheepskin jacket.

Richard's eyes followed them to the bar; his glass had been empty for a while. As they were waiting to be served, Max greeted an Italian man who'd just arrived. The man kissed Lucia on both cheeks and then stood close to Max.

But we know him! Merlo said, nudging Lars and pointing across the room at the new arrival.

He lives in the flat above us, Lars explained.

That's a coincidence, Richard said.

Not really, Merlo said. Venice is a glorified village.

Max, Lucia and the new arrival made their way back. Max walked carefully, with brimming glasses pressed together in his hands – his friend walked behind, holding small plates of squid and artichokes and slices of bread, with knives and forks wrapped in napkins clumped together in his other hand.

Max placed the drinks together in the centre of the table, and his friend put the plates and cutlery down next to them. Per tutti, he said, then pointed at himself. Tommaso. Piacere. Neat brown hair and a goatee; a dark-green corduroy suit; a Barbour jacket. A few years older than everyone else.

You are very autumnal, Lucia said, pronouncing the last word deliberately and looking at Richard for approval.

Richard didn't know where Max and Tommaso had met. He didn't think Tommaso was an archive person – although he couldn't be sure, because nowadays Richard rolled in at noon, just in time to get a request in before they stopped fetching files. Then he transcribed documents for a couple of hours without really reading them – until he felt he'd done his duty and left early.

You live above us, Merlo said to Tommaso.

We saw you on the roof, Lars said.

The cat, Tommaso said to Richard. It goes up and can't get down.

Lars said, We were coming home with shopping, and I was trying to find my keys. And oh, there's a man up there wearing a helmet and a harness. Lars looked up towards the ceiling of Paradiso and wiped his expression clean by passing the palm of his hand in front of it. Then he waved at an imaginary man up in the rafters. Hi!

And I wave back, Tommaso said. Not exactly, because I have the cat in one hand and the other on a rope.

How did you manage to get onto the roof? Richard asked Tommaso, when everyone had rearranged themselves around the table and sat down.

There's an altana, and my mother forgets to close the skylight. That's how the cat gets out, but it won't come back, so I have to go farther out, where the roof slopes. It's not dangerous, but I wear the climbing gear to stop my mother from worrying.

I've never noticed the altana.

You are welcome to use it. There's not much point now, but it's a good place to sunbathe in summer.

I don't think Riccardo has ever sunbathed in his life, Merlo said. She'd taken to calling him by the Italian version of his name – emphasising the *k* sound in the middle and rolling both *r*s.

Well, I feel differently about sunlight nowadays, Richard said. But maybe not enough to get my skin burned off.

Max told me you both take photographs, Tommaso said.

Yes, Richard said, waving the rangefinder towards Tommaso, but she cheats. She brings her own light.

What does it say on the back of your camera?

Richard looked down at the handwritten note he'd taped to the camera body. It says, *Meter reads one stop too high.* To remind me.

We have a couple of prints in our apartment: Gianni Berengo Gardin, Letizia Battaglia. My mother buys art when she can.

We'd love to see them, Merlo said.

We can go later, Tommaso said.

Won't your mother mind?

She's out late. There's a conference at the university.

What does she do? Lars asked.

She is a professor of history. Not Venetian history – the Ottoman Empire.

Everyone ate and made appreciative noises to say thank you to Max and Tommaso.

I never had squid before I came to Venice, Lars said.

Never mind squid, Richard said. I never had artichokes. Posh food.

You don't have to be posh to eat well, Merlo said. You just have to care about what you put in your mouth.

Is posh the same as bourgeois? Lucia asked.

Not exactly, Richard said.

It's true that Venice is a bourgeois place, Tommaso said. Conservative. He straightened his back. But for me, this is ordinary food.

Paradiso doesn't feel especially conservative, Richard said.

Sporco bars, though, Lars said.

Sporco? Tommaso said.

It's what Lars and me call them, Richard said. Not really dirty. Squalido.

Not squalido either, Lars said. The unlit cigarette in his mouth jiggled up and down.

But definitely not posh, Richard added.

Only guys, Lars said. Maybe there's a woman making the sandwiches from a giant, sweaty mortadella.

Strip lights. Always too bright. So a good place to photograph, if you're feeling brave. Which you'd better be.

No price list. Well, there is, but only for us.

They know who's Venetian and who isn't, Richard said to Merlo.

Venice is an open place, porous, Tommaso said, but it's also closed. It protects itself against invaders.

'Ariva i barbari', Merlo said.

Ah, you know the song.

Were you born here?

We moved when I was twelve. So I'm an invader too.

On the way back to Tommaso's apartment, everyone progressed like ships in convoy, cut back to the speed of the slowest participant. In this case, Lucia, who walked arm in arm with Max and Tommaso on either side of her. Their group got in the way of other people trying to pass on the Fondamenta, and there was a lot of shuffling about when the street got narrower. Richard found all this irritating and sped up, so he ended up scouting ahead. Groups were far more self-absorbed than people walking alone, but their self-regard was mutually reinforcing, so they didn't notice.

When Richard reached the cortile where Lars and Merlo lived, he stopped and waited, since he didn't know which entrance led to Tommaso's apartment. When Tommaso arrived, he went to a door with polished brass handles. Venite, he said, beckoning them all into the hall behind, where there was a stone staircase leading up.

On the landing of the staircase, there was a neat row of wellington boots. That's random, Richard said.

There's no point putting them down below, Tommaso said. Because when you need them, they're underwater.

The inner door of Tommaso's flat opened onto a large portego, with whitewashed walls and a terrazzo floor, though it was just as uneven as the one in Merlo's apartment. Tommaso turned the light on: a Murano chandelier with several flame-shaped bulbs, but only half of them worked, so the illumination didn't quite reach the room's corners. The walls were covered with pictures and prints, and there was even a bronze bust of a man in spectacles perched on top of a writing desk overflowing with letters and bills. Lars walked over to the statue and touched the glasses, which must have been cast separately and then fixed to the face. My mother's uncle, Tommaso said, without explaining further.

Who made it? Lars asked.

I don't know. We inherited it. Tommaso walked over to a section of the wall where framed photographs hung in a row at head height. This is the Berengo Gardin, he said, standing in front of the first print on the left.

I know this one, Richard said. It's in all his books.

My mother bought it many years ago, before I was born. We probably could not afford it now.

The photograph showed the interior of a vaporetto divided by reflections and doors into a series of Cubist superimpositions of bodies and heads and faces.

No women, Merlo said.

I think the passengers are all on their way to work, Tommaso said. He moved along the row of prints. This is the Battaglia.

A frontal portrait of a woman with her eyes closed, split in two vertically by a deep shadow line, so that half of her face was lost in darkness.

You have to know the story, Tommaso said. She is at her husband's funeral – he was one of Falcone's bodyguards. They all died with him when the bomb went off.

Actual crime-scene photos, Merlo said, nudging Richard.

Battaglia does those as well, yes, Tommaso said. Too brutal to put on your wall.

I don't want dead bodies, Richard said to Merlo. That's like photographing celebrities or sunsets.

What do you mean? Tommaso said.

In the Berengo Gardin: this is interesting *because I say so*. Not because it's news. Not because everyone else says it's interesting.

Nobody wanted to look at what Battaglia was photographing, Merlo said. The mafia threatened her. She did it anyway.

Well, obviously she's better than me.

Me too.

But it's still journalism.

It has a purpose, yes, but that's not a bad thing.

It's true that my mother bought this to commemorate a moment in Italian history, Tommaso said. When the mafia blew Falcone up – suddenly it was out in the open, and it felt like it might change.

They already have streets named after him, Lucia said.

And did things change? Richard asked.

Tommaso shrugged. Then he pointed at the rest of the prints and said, The others are mainly family photos.

How far back do they go?

My great-grandparents, in Liguria.

Richard wasn't sure if this included the father's side of the family. Tommaso hadn't mentioned him.

I love these old studio photos with weird props, Merlo said. Classical columns, backdrops.

What do you photograph, then? Tommaso asked Richard.

He thought about this for a moment. The city I'm living in, he said.

As opposed to the one you're studying in the archive?

We all pretend Venice hasn't changed. I did too, when I first got here – but I can't do it any more.

He wanted to become part of history, instead of remaining forever outside, nose pressed to the glass. History didn't stop four hundred years ago – it kept going, until it reached Richard, here, in December 2000.

But that's a problem, he said.

Why? Tommaso asked.

Because it's not what I'm here for.

You're wrong, Merlo said. It *is* what you're here for.

How about you? Tommaso asked her.

I photograph different things. At the moment – my friends. That's interesting enough.

You make it interesting, Richard said. He realised that Tommaso had only volunteered information about his mother, nothing about himself – so he said, And what do you do?

Me? Oh, I haven't decided yet. Perhaps I would like to be an art dealer.

Can we go up on the altana? Lucia asked.

It's cold now, and there's not much to see at night.

The view at night is more interesting, Richard said.

Okay then. Sure.

The flat had two short corridors leading off the portego. Tommaso led them to the one on the left, which had a door to the kitchen, another to a small toilet and shower, and a wooden staircase leading up to an attic.

We use this as a guest room, Tommaso said, when they'd all reached the top of the stairs. The attic had a sloping roof and skylight, and a ladder that led through the skylight onto a wooden viewing platform. It took a couple of minutes to get everyone up there on the ladder. Richard followed Lars: he could see the frayed waistband of his greying Calvin Kleins where they poked over the top of his jeans.

Up on the platform, Richard swung around in a circle with the rangefinder to his eye. But Tommaso was right: there wasn't much to see. Certainly not the Grand Canal or San Marco: nearby roofs to the south, and, to the north, a screen of darkness pricked by a few navigation lights on boats in the lagoon. Then a glittering smear on the horizon for Murano, and another farther away for the airport.

On a clear day, you can see the Dolomiti, Tommaso said.

I can *hear* the lagoon, Lucia said. And smell the salt.

I can smell someone smoking a joint, Richard said.

Not guilty, Lars said.

The altana platform was only about three metres square, so it was crowded with six of them up there.

I can make coffee if you like, Tommaso said, gesturing towards the ladder.

Lucia went down first, stepping carefully in reverse in her low heels. The others followed, until Merlo and Richard were alone on the altana.

Do you remember *Wings of Desire?* Richard said.

Come down from on high. Get face to face.

I don't have any photographs of my family.

None?

My dad might have some – but I don't see him. I couldn't even tell you what my grandparents did. I don't have a history. That's why I came here: to borrow other people's.

You can have mine, Merlo said. I don't mind sharing.

NEGATIVE 123/16:
PIAZZA SAN MARCO, 1/60S

At the bar in an overpriced café. The waiter knows I'm not going to tip him, but he keeps his contempt to himself. Behind me, way back over my right shoulder, framed by curtains, there's a plate-glass window, which looks onto a colonnade. Because it's dark outside, a projection of the waiter's face bounces back off the plate glass into the café interior. All that's reflected in the mirror behind the bar.

People walking past the window on the street outside always glance in. It's a reflex; they can't help it. So if I set the focal point of my lens 'inside' the mirror, I can capture someone looking through the glass, from outside the café, at the exact moment they pass the outline of the waiter, projected onto the window from inside the café. A reflection, next to the reflection of a reflection.

Since I'm left-handed, when I look through the viewfinder it covers my left eye. I have to press the camera body in tight against my glasses and the bridge of my nose; and then I have to pull it away to flip the film lever forwards. Before I release the shutter, I hold my breath, because when the air leaves my lungs, my hands will shake. So each exposure is a single breath, contained, and that makes it a single perception, discrete, with a duration – in this case, one-sixtieth of a second. The slowest I can risk, given the person outside will be in motion.

This image is a hypothesis in my head before it's an experiment, and it's a singular experiment, unrepeatable. I'll have to bring the camera up fast and shove it in the waiter's face, no warning. He'll put up with that, even without the tip, but I won't get away with it twice.

When someone outside is about two seconds away from the right location, before they become visible in the mirror, the sound of their footsteps reaches a particular pitch. That's my cue. Start moving the camera up to my eye when I hear it, before the image is ready, before it presents itself.

Click.

One-sixtieth of a second is — just, barely — long enough to distinguish the sound of the shutter opening from the sound of its closing. In that interval, I see nothing, I'm conscious of nothing — except duration itself.

No one ever asks the next question, the obvious question: How did you keep yourself out of the mirror?

8

THIS TIME WHEN RICHARD RETURNED FROM VENICE THERE was a letter from the Scottish Office, who paid his scholarship, warning him he needed to make definite progress by the end of the academic year. For his first-year evaluation, he'd submitted a revamped version of his doctoral proposal, which fooled no one. There was also a letter from his supervisor in his pigeonhole – in a noticeably less friendly tone than previous communications – instructing him to check in, and a more neutral note from the lecturer who ran the graduate history seminar, who'd been on the evaluation panel, inviting him to give a paper on his research.

There was also a sympathy card with an enclosed note from his foster mum, and a long letter on thick, headed notepaper from a solicitor in Liverpool, informing him his dad had died. These last two had been here for several weeks – he hadn't left any contact details for Venice, and his foster mum didn't use email. So he'd missed the funeral.

He hadn't seen his dad for – what was it, two years? That was probably Richard's fault. His mum had left under mysterious circumstances when he was ten, and his dad worked abroad in the merchant navy. So Richard lived with his dad's sister in Liverpool for a couple of years, and then, when his aunt moved away, and his dad didn't appear to collect him one day at the scheduled time, he went into the group home. Eventually he ended up with his foster mum. He occasionally saw his dad on visits. Richard supposed he loved his foster mum – but he didn't like her touching him.

He didn't feel anything when he read the card and the letter, but for a week he took more tablets than usual and got drunk every night. Peeled himself out of bed in the mornings and locked himself in the college darkroom. The pure smell of the chemicals disguised the alcoholic sweat.

His dad didn't own much, not even a car. His remaining effects were at the solicitor's in a few boxes, which Richard had no intention of collecting. But there was an insurance policy, so there was some money. Half of it went to Richard's aunt – presumably an agreement with her in return for looking after him years ago. Even so, the solicitor's letter enclosed a cheque for several thousand pounds. When it had cleared, Richard bought a second-hand large-format camera that used individual sheets of film, four-by-five inches. It dated from the 1980s, but the design was the same as the one Atget used in Paris a century ago. The body had a varnished cherry-wood frame, a bellows, and a ground-glass screen at the back. You had to unfold the camera like an accordion to set it up on the tripod, and then flap a cloth over your head so you could make out the image on the screen. The frame had cheap alloy fittings you could bend with your hand, but that didn't matter – only the lens on the front and the film at the back.

Richard spent most of his time in Cambridge practising how to use this camera, or printing the negatives from his last trip to Venice, but he accepted the invitation to give a paper in the hope that it would pacify his supervisor. He postponed it until the end of the summer term, and then wrote it all at the last minute. He was supposed to talk about surveillance, but that wasn't what came out.

The graduate seminar took place in a stuffy upstairs room off the main quad in King's. Outside, workmen were clanking and banging scaffolding to set up stages for the May Ball. In the room, a grandfather clock echoed down to doomsday. Sitting at the head of the table, waiting for the other postgrads to arrive, Richard drew figures in the margins of the printed page in front of him: men in wigs and ruffs being stabbed and shot, ejecting gouts of black blood in protest. A speech balloon from a floating, decapitated head: *I remember when all this was new.*

He'd taken a temazepam, and as he moved the leaking biro in his left hand up in front of his face, he marvelled at the hand's steadiness, then watched it descend to deposit the pen by the side of his small stack of pages. The empty hand now flattened itself down onto the surface of the top sheet of paper, but it couldn't be trusted: it left a damp mark that wrinkled the page.

Richard's face was red and he wanted to take his jumper off, but he was scared there were sweat stains under his arms. He'd asked for a slide projector, and he concentrated on the way the struggling fan interacted with the pendulum of the grandfather clock and the more random interjections of the workmen outside. This distracted him from the murmured conversation of new arrivals, who gradually filled up the empty chairs.

Dr Christiansen, the lecturer who ran the seminar, sat beside him with her glasses pushed up into her greying bobbed hair, reading a printout: perhaps a submission from one of her students. That pile of pages was much thicker than the one in front of Richard.

He looked behind him at the image already floating on the screen: a slide of a photo by Shōmei Tōmatsu from 1961 titled *A wrist-watch dug up approximately 0.7 km from the epicentre of the explosion, Nagasaki*. The time on the watch was the minute when the atomic bomb dropped on the morning of 9 August 1945: two minutes past eleven. Richard moved his arm through the projector's beam – watched the shadow of his hand open and close in front of the image.

An American woman Richard had met during his MA year hovered in the corner of his eye – was she doing something on Tudor masculinity? When he turned around to acknowledge her presence, she said, I just wanted to tell you, good luck. Then she sat down in the seat nearest to him, opposite Dr Christiansen.

Thanks, he said. Had she been one of Camille's friends?

When Dr Christiansen introduced Richard, she paused for a moment before reading out the title of the paper, as if she wasn't sure she'd got it right: 'History and Photography'. The room was half-full: about fifteen people. More than Richard had expected, given he'd chosen the last slot on the calendar. As he was about to begin, his supervisor, Professor Matlock, slipped in at the back and sat down. He was carrying his cycle helmet and he still had the clips on his trouser bottoms, as if he was planning a quick getaway. His glasses made his eyes enormous, like he was peering across the room through binoculars into Richard's soul. There were two of Professor Matlock's other students in the room – maybe more. He had a lot of supervisees, and Richard hadn't been introduced to all of them. That information seemed to be distributed on a need-to-know basis.

Richard placed his finger over the first word on the page in front of him and closed his eyes. Then said the invisible word aloud: Bang. He opened his eyes and read on, now following the printed lines on the page: The aftermath of an explosion, detritus all over a bomb site, blackened components picked out and arranged on plastic sheets. History is born here, out of still-smouldering ashes and fragments whose trajectory is only finally arrested in the historian's flesh.

So far, so Walter Benjamin.

He gestured towards the image on the screen behind him, and continued: The dead touch the living only insofar as the living identify with their death, receiving the past as stigmata, which means receiving it simultaneously as a representation and a direct emanation of the original wound.

History means learning how to die by imitation: reliving death. It means bearing witness, as the body of Saint Francis bore witness to the Passion of Christ.

He pressed the remote controller for the projector; the screen went black momentarily before the carousel turned and another Tōmatsu photograph clunked noisily into view: *Memory of Defeat 2, Ruins of Toyokawa Naval Dockyard, Aichi Prefecture*. A rusting wall at an abandoned military site, punctured by shrapnel holes, and backlit, so the puncture wounds glowed, as if there was still a fire burning behind the wall.

Richard read, History means reading your own fate in the entrails of the dead, in the constellations formed on the retina by burning spots of time.

Someone at the back of the room coughed; someone else whispered to their neighbour, who shifted in his seat. Richard glanced at his supervisor, who was looking out the sash window, down at the workmen in the quad.

A black and white image is burned onto the negative, Richard said. Scar tissue. A colour image, by contrast, bleeds onto the negative. It is a bruise, and the dyes from which it is formed are exaggerated, artificial versions of the hues of a bruise: purple, blue and yellow, whilst the chemicals used to fix the print are blood-red.

He flashed up a Shakespeare quotation on a slide behind him – as if it too was an image – and read it aloud: *The paper as the body of my friend, And every word in it a gaping wound Issuing life blood.*

It is easy to forget, he continued, that parchment is made of skin until you come across imperfectly cured pages, and the smell of bad meat impregnates the fingers along with flaking gilt.

He paused to wipe his mouth, as if he needed a moment to gather his thoughts, but he really wanted to reassure himself with the smell of chemicals from the darkroom, which hung around his hands constantly now.

He continued, And it is not just parchment that carries the taint. In the early seventeenth century, paper was made from scraps of clothing gathered by rag-and-bone men. During periods of plague, the Venetian government was terrified that unscrupulous individuals would use garments stripped from the victims for this purpose, in which case the documents would quite literally be contaminated by death.

He paused again, although he hated these performative gestures when he wasn't sitting up here at the front. You 'gave' a 'paper', which meant reading out a pre-existing written text, so the most authentic performance would be to deliver it in an uninterrupted, breathless monotone – which, indeed, some people did. Or not to read it aloud at all: project the entire thing on the screen behind you, page by page and slide by slide, and let people read it silently to themselves. Why did anyone need to be here at all? An archaic trial by combat.

He'd considered projecting photos of the text of his paper as he read it, but with handwritten corrections and erasures, their number gradually increasing so that the final page was entirely scribbled out. Maybe he could even try to compose another text out of the uncensored words, ideally one whose argument contradicted the one he was reading aloud.

A loud clang outside as a workman dropped something, followed by angry shouts. In the room, someone's mobile phone started ringing, and they rummaged in their bag for several seconds before managing to turn it off.

Sorry!

Richard continued with several more minutes of mystical waffle about ruins, before finally getting to the point: What, in fact, does the archive record, and how? It is useful here to compare documents with photographs. Susan Sontag says that a photograph is a trace, a stencil; she compares it to a death mask. Writing works quite differently to this. It's more like a painting: it always interprets rather than shows. In light of this (so to speak) – he hated this kind of prissy, self-congratulatory play on words – Roland Barthes notes the irony of the simultaneous invention of photography and academic history in the nineteenth century. Both made the same claim to reproduce a past reality, but only photography was able to fulfil it – and, moreover, in ways that ultimately undermined rather than reinforced history's claims. In contrast to the attempt by nineteenth-century historians to find a grand design and pattern in the past, photography works by isolating fragments and juxtaposing them, chopping up time rather than presenting it as a unified whole. The world implied by the photograph is, as Sontag puts it, inherently surreal and discontinuous, animated by contradictions.

Sontag, Barthes – the unacknowledged presence of Walter Benjamin – was that enough name-dropping? Shōmei Tōmatsu didn't count; no one was impressed by people they hadn't heard of. He hated this too: genuflecting at altars and crossing yourself, in case the presiding saint decided to curse you for failing to acknowledge them.

He clicked through to the next slide, which showed one of his photos of Venice – but he didn't explain that fact or even refer to the image. Nonetheless, he said, while wiping his palms under the table against his trousers, there is a sense in which documents resemble photographs. A document becomes a direct emanation rather than an interpretation if we consider it as evidence of its own production.

In other words, a document records the action or event of somebody writing something down. We know that on a certain date a decision was recorded in a file, a petition was registered with a court, a will was drawn up, a court secretary wrote down the words of a witness; and so on.

He didn't believe his own argument here. Photographs weren't merely a record of the photographer's decision to trip the shutter. They also pointed outwards, towards the world – otherwise what was the point? But he was marking out a defensible position in anticipation of attack.

But documents are also aesthetic objects, whose precise formal properties render them beautiful, and their worth partly derives from their beauty as objects – even ruined, decayed or defaced objects.

Why was he so obsessed with decay?

More grandiose generalisations intercut with images of Venice, then a return to mystical waffle in the final paragraph of his printout: The archive provides the means to treat the wound that it inflicts. It is a memorial as well as a morgue. It is where we learn to grieve. Death inoculates against death.

What did that even mean? Anyway, it was over now. He turned the last page over to its blank side and unhunched his shoulders. As he picked up his bottle of water with his now shaking hand, he realised: for all his grand pronouncements about the archive, he hadn't quoted a single Venetian document. Except the photographs – they were his documents. But they were pristine: the prints anyway. The images themselves were sometimes blurred and grainy, but even in those, he was still trying to make a coherent statement; to fight against the chaos, not give in to it.

He'd got it wrong. He wasn't interested in ruins and decay. That was where he'd begun, with the Polaroids. But now he was interested in restoration. A reverse anachronism: using obsolete things to extend the present backwards.

Normally, Dr Christiansen made some attempt to summarise the paper, but today she moved straight on to questions.

The sweep of the ticking clock reasserted its dominance of the room over the complaint of the projector fan. Richard remembered a medieval history seminar in Glasgow where a student gave a presentation on Eleanor of Aquitaine, but wrote it like she was the heroine of a romance novel. The silence after that talk was like this one.

A mature student with wild hair finally said, How can you justify what you've just done?

Someone laughed – Richard wasn't sure if it was directed at him or the questioner, who wasn't popular.

I think you have the burden of proof wrong, he said. I'm not required to justify it. You're required to tell me why I *can't* do it.

Bravado. They were about to cut his funding off, so he *was* required to justify it. But he might as well go down swinging.

Another long pause – maybe because Richard had broken the rules by dismissing the question. Then the American woman who'd wished him luck said, What if I accept all this? What kind of history would I write?

You'd take photographs, Richard thought, but he wasn't sure he'd actually argued that. So he said, It would be more like archaeology: the document as an excavated object. And more like art history: the document as a work of art. What does it look like, feel like? How was it made?

I was thinking about the form of the writing itself, she said. *Your* writing.

Richard quoted Benjamin: *History decomposes into images, not stories.* Or stories about images.

The *Arcades Project* is a collage of quotations.

Photographs are quotations too. I mean, context is king – all the talks I've ever heard in this room, more and more context. That's the definition of good history. But what if you pry something loose instead? Cut it out; put a frame around it.

But he does provide the context. Benjamin. He does it by accumulation and montage.

Sure. You're right.

A man who worked on the French Wars of Religion put his hand up and waited for Dr Christiansen to call on him. He said, All your … metaphors were about chemical photography. So what happens to your argument if you switch to digital?

It's a good question, but I think it's for someone else. Because I've got no intention of switching.

Laughter.

Exposure, development, negative, darkroom. I don't know what the equivalent metaphors are for digital. I mean, it's very laborious, printing in a darkroom – expensive too. It's ridiculous to be doing that *because it's a good metaphor*. And yet, here I am.

Dr Christiansen said, What I want to know: how did you get here from researching spies?

Well, I thought photography would teach me something about spying. That's what Sontag says: all photographers are voyeurs. But I discovered something different. I'm part of the world you see in the photographs.

They're yours then?

The ones I didn't attribute to someone else, yes.

I honestly can't see how this can lead to you being awarded a PhD in early modern history – maybe if you switched to modern. Or philosophy of history.

But it's too late for that, Richard said.

Dr Christiansen smiled in sympathy.

Professor Matlock stood up and left the room. Richard watched him leave. So did everyone else.

When the questions had finished and people were talking and packing up, Dr Christiansen leaned over and said, I have a friend, in London. He runs a small press who do photography books. I don't know if he'd be interested – but Venice is popular, and they look good to me. I'm happy to drop him a line.

Thank you.

Do you have scans I can email?

I can get some.

You're coming to the Eagle?

I don't think so. I have work to do.

Don't assume what people thought. You might be surprised.

Richard shook his head. I know it didn't make sense, he said. But he understood what she was saying: *Don't run away; don't be a coward.* He wasn't running away, though. He was going back to the darkroom – back to Venice.

His end-of-year evaluation was scheduled for late October, at the beginning of his third year. That meant he'd already have the advance payment for that term from the Scottish Office. And he still had three thousand pounds from his inheritance.

A week after the seminar, he booked a flight to Venice for early September. No point even going to the evaluation. He'd just assume he'd failed.

NEGATIVE 224/34:
SANTA MARIA DELLA SALUTE, 1/125S

A pickpocket: one definition of the photographer. Steals your image, steals your soul. An old idea, a myth. A story we tell ourselves to explain why photography bothers us. We give the belief to other cultures, because we're not so foolish, oh no – but it's our anxiety really. We're scared to be who we appear to be. We're scared that's all our 'soul' is: an appearance.

It works like this. I'm special. I'm a riddle, and my appearance is a clue, which I leave behind without wanting to, like a fingerprint. I can't stop manifesting a symptom, which the photographer diagnoses. So my appearance is a weakness, a vulnerability, an 'exposure'.

Thirty-seven tourists. An encyclopaedia of all the responses anyone might possibly make to the presence of a camera. Except, they're not responding to the camera.

An improvised theatrical performance is about to start behind me. I'm ignoring the show, pointedly, my back to it, as a man on stilts reaches down to take my hat. As I press the shutter release, I'm failing to catch him in the act. That's what the crowd's reacting to: my impending humiliation. They're sharing a joke, but not with me, and not with the camera.

The shutter blinks; my hat goes up. The man on stilts wants me to chase him, make it last longer. Revenge for turning my back. A quick calculation: I'd rather lose the hat. He can see this, so he hands it back down.

Smile. Make another calculation, a bet with karma. In exchange for a petty humiliation, you'll receive a great photograph. Take the bet, every time. Thirty-seven faces bear witness to this promise.

That's what I think I've discovered, walking away, clutching my hat. But humiliation isn't humility. Bargains with fate are all very well. Fate isn't listening, doesn't give a shit. The real lesson is simpler: I'm not in control.

Stop fighting. My appearance is not an involuntary betrayal of myself. I become legible, in the photograph, even when I'm behind the camera. Who am I? A fool without a hat, facing the wrong way.

9

RICHARD COULD HEAR HIM COMING ALONG THE LONG GANG-
way bolted onto the north side of the Arsenale wall. The man began
screaming when he stepped onto the gangway's far end, and he continued at twenty-second intervals during his approach, but the only
escape for a quarter of a mile in either direction was the long drop to
the sea below, and Richard was in the middle of a seventeen-minute
exposure, so he stayed where he was and hoped for the best.

There were actually two of them – but the other one was sober.
What you doing? the shouter asked when he got close. Eastern
European, maybe Polish.

Richard was never sure how to answer this question. Sometimes
he went for the literal *Taking a photo*, but that led to *What of?*, which
led to *What for?*, and he didn't want to prolong this conversation,
so he said, I'm working. He kept his back to both of them and his
arms spread out to protect the camera, like he was its bodyguard.

Working! Ha! I'm working too.

Via, his friend said, moving past. *Come on.*

The drunk swayed, then stepped delicately around the tripod leg.

Richard had gone out to the Bacini a couple of hours before. The
vaporetto didn't stop there after dark unless you asked. Qui? said the
man handling the ropes. Sei sicuro? No one else was getting off, and
there were only a handful of other passengers huddled in the rear
cabin. Standing alone on the dock, Richard watched the vaporetto
pull away, the windows glowing against the surrounding darkness
and the cabin light picking out the crests of the waves.

The Bacini were modern shipyards at Venice's northeast corner, surrounded by CCTV cameras and yellow warning triangles, though Richard wasn't convinced there was anything inside worth protecting. When did they last build a ship there? Maybe they still did repairs. When he got close to the outer wall, he triggered a floodlight and he could hear a dog barking on the other side.

If you kept to the main streets in Venice, the routes trod out by millions of feet, the city felt welcoming – like it was posing for the camera – and no one bothered you except other tourists. But there was a different city, made up of areas demolished, redeveloped, then abandoned again. A city of derelict factories, half-empty warehouses and offices – a city behind spiked gates and walls with barbed wire on top. On the map, these areas often showed as blank, but as soon as you stepped close to their borders, then, at that precise moment, as if by magic, a sullen security guard unfamiliar with the concept of public space appeared.

Richard took a couple of steps backwards – the floodlight pinged off, the dog fell silent – but it would take half an hour to set the large-format camera up, and it wasn't worth the risk to photograph a dead wall. So he retreated back towards the Arsenale. He set up and exposed a couple of sheets in the interzone between the restricted area and a makeshift slum, where restaurant and hotel workers lived. Then he fell back again to the gangway, the only way to reach the Bacini on foot, and the only route in or out at all once the vaporettos stopped running.

There were two typical spaces in Venice: the open campo, with a parish church; and the narrow enclosed alleys surrounding and linking the campi, bricks rising up on either side, storey after storey. Neither of these spaces interested Richard. He'd photographed in the alleys two years ago with the Spectra, but if you wanted to represent them as three-dimensional, they didn't give you much choice. Telephoto or wide-angle, point the camera up or down: always the same – one-point perspective, plunging away from the lens.

The gangway along the Arsenale wall was like an alley – but cut in half vertically down the middle, with one side removed and exposed to the sea. A cross-section of an alley. Maybe that was interesting.

He went to the middle of the gangway, where it rose into a bridge to accommodate the north water exit from the Arsenale. He couldn't see anything on the camera's ground-glass screen at night except the bulbs of streetlights, so he had to use the ones in the distance to figure out where the horizon was. Then he placed a torch on the ground to determine where the bottom of the frame cut off, by moving the light backwards and forwards, then returning to the back of the camera to check when and where its pinprick disappeared – off the top of the screen, since the image was upside down and back to front.

There was no focusing scale on the camera, and he couldn't see well enough to set the focus visually, so he racked the bellows out to somewhere a few metres ahead, and stopped the lens down. But a small aperture meant a long exposure.

Still shit. The same boring, fuck-off brick, continuing for infinity.

Once he'd packed up the camera, he walked back along the gangway towards the lights, and came back onto the waterfront north of where he stayed with Max last year. He'd moved for this trip to an apartment near Merlo and Lars in Cannaregio. He'd seen a notice on the board at the Graduate Centre in Cambridge: an Italian student subletting, probably making a nice income on the side. He kept walking along the Fondamente Nove, then turned left into the city, past the new cinema and Bianco e Nero, where he still got his negatives developed. Because he had the rucksack on his back, there wasn't enough space for the tripod strap on his shoulder, so he walked hunched up to try to stop it slipping off, but he still had to keep twitching the damn thing back into place. A prosthetic tic.

During this final visit to Venice, he alternated working with the large-format camera, the rangefinder and the Rolleiflex. Most photographers used one camera, one format – but in 1936, when Walker Evans documented the lives of sharecroppers in the American South, he took formal portraits with his large-format camera, and while the subjects got ready, washing and combing and so on, he shot them handheld on 35mm. It was like alternating between sprint and long-distance: using different muscles, forcing yourself to rethink your assumptions, your approach. Ideally, Richard would have liked to set up the large-format camera somewhere, and then, while the shutter was open for however long the exposure took, usually fifteen minutes or more, he'd use the rangefinder to photograph people moving through the same space and around the camera on the tripod. He couldn't quite manage to split his attention like that in the moment, so he divided it up over the day instead.

He woke up hungover; in the afternoons, he went out on the vaporettos, up and down the Grand Canal, or farther out, to the islands, where he walked around with the Rolleiflex; after dinner, he started work with the large-format camera. As the evening went on, he got tenser and tenser, but that suited the camera, everything clenched and locked. When he took the first drink, he switched back to 35mm and photographed in the bars – being slightly drunk worked there. Then, at home, he had an hour or two to dissolve and let go of the day. Admit to himself he'd done nothing of value. It was all shit – but there was always tomorrow.

His apartment was past Enzo's bar, near Campo Sant'Alvise, inside a courtyard and up an external staircase to a door on the first floor. Richard had never had a place to himself before. In Glasgow, he'd stayed in bedsits, and the college accommodation in Cambridge all had shared kitchens and bathrooms. This flat had what felt like an ocean of space: a bedroom, a kitchen, a separate lounge. But he spent a lot of his time in the short corridor between the bedroom and the kitchen, because that was where the gas heater was fixed to the wall, with an exhaust flue disappearing up into the ceiling.

The bathroom only had lace curtains, and the windows looked onto the courtyard, so at night he didn't turn the light on, just fumbled his way around using the reflected light from the corridor. He hadn't had much space in his luggage on this trip, because of the large-format camera, so he didn't have many clothes, and only one pair of pyjamas. When he got in, they were still wet from the wash, so he laid them steaming on the metal cover of the heater. He'd done this several times before, and he didn't always get the timing right, so they now had scorch marks, which were becoming holes. It didn't matter – he'd throw them away when he left Venice.

He dumped his camera gear in the lounge and brought a chair, a glass and a plastic bottle of water from the kitchen – along with a half-full bottle of whisky. It wasn't too expensive if you bought it in supermarkets. He sat down to watch his pyjamas cook, and turn them over occasionally.

A pall of failure still hung around him from Cambridge, and he hadn't managed to photograph his way out of it. He couldn't escape the knowledge of what was waiting for him there when he went back.

Just after he'd arrived in Venice, two planes had flown into the World Trade Center in New York. That evening he'd gone to eat cicchetti in Alla Botte near Rialto, and the television screen above the bar had replayed the footage endlessly, the hysterical commentary in Italian too fast for him to follow. The place was crowded: people holding on to each other but staring up at the screen, mouths open and tears in their eyes. No proper conversations, only fragments of phrases and sounds of dismay. He had the rangefinder with him, and he thought maybe he ought to photograph these reactions – it was part of what was happening – but he couldn't do it. Like photographing at your friend's funeral.

There was a photo on the wall in Alla Botte, which showed the aftermath of the infamous Pink Floyd concert in Piazza San Marco in 1989, everything covered in a tide of garbage. And a caption underneath: *Never again!* But you couldn't stop the tide of history from swallowing you – not unless you were an angel floating above the city.

The feeling from that day had stayed with him, although he knew it was a version of the pathetic fallacy. The world wasn't falling apart to validate his personal crisis. He wasn't on fire, jumping from the umpteenth floor of a collapsing building. He still had the responsibility of imagining a future for himself.

A scratch on his cornea was dancing. Off-centre, so every time he flicked his eye towards it, the scratch moved too, farther into peripheral vision. It swam blindly back and forth, revealing the extent of his eye movements as it did so. He stared up at the bulb in the corridor ceiling. Last night, a tiny fly had skipped through its penumbra. Too fast to register its individual movements. He could only infer them during the brief intervals it rested on the ceiling. Inspired by the heat of the bulb. Magic. The dancing scratch inside his eye was magic too. He couldn't stop it moving, or even isolate the focal plane on which it sat. Multiple scratches, he now saw. Not scratches: stains. Some kind of macular degeneration. Different from the afterglow of the bulb, or the teeming sparks when you blinked, or the patterns formed by firing neurons when you pressed your fingertips against your closed lids. Floating black wisps, like sunspots.

He peeled his pyjamas off the heater and chucked them through the door of his bedroom, then went back to the chair in the hallway.

He couldn't image a future until he imagined his past. He closed his eyes and forced himself to think about Camille: locked himself back inside her room in Cambridge. No escape – not until the image was fully developed.

On the last night he spoke to her, she undid her coat and scarf; flung them onto her chair and flopped forwards onto her bed. Oof, she said, bouncing face down on the mattress.

Richard sat down next to her, manipulating the springs, becoming her echo. Her fingers were half an inch from his. The gap between them was alive, seething.

I can see it in you, she said. I used to have a dog. He was the same. He'd pull on the lead tighter and tighter, until he began to choke. He'd keep pulling, choking himself, until I jerked him back. Then he'd quiet down for a few seconds, and start again. Just walk at the right distance! The lead is never going to get longer, however hard you pull.

I'm not your dog, Richard lied, swaying into the rhythm of an alcoholic pulsation. There was a hum in the air, a violent evacuation like the interval between a lightning fork and a thunderclap.

Camille said, I want you to touch me.

She was still lying face down on the bed. Her skirt bunched up, woollen tights underneath. He ran the backs of his fingers along the back of her legs, then placed a hand around each thigh. She didn't close her legs; she didn't open them either. He folded her skirt up above her waist. He placed his fingers inside the elastic rim of her tights and pulled downwards.

She wriggled her hips. White cotton knickers. He pulled them aside. One finger inside, then two. Slow.

No, she said, but she was wet and he didn't believe her.

He moved his fingers again.

No, she said. I can't. Not looking at him.

He stopped. He said, You asked me to touch you.

She twitched. No I didn't.

What? You said, 'I want you to touch me.'

I didn't say that.

He removed himself from her. Wiping his fingers on her seemed unchivalrous; his own trouser leg would do.

I didn't say anything, she repeated.

So I'm making it up?

Another pulsation.

A blackout? But he lost short-term memory in a blackout; he didn't create imaginary experiences. He held his hand to his mouth, as if stifling a gasp, or the urge to vomit. The same hand that was inside Camille a moment ago. Drowning in her.

He stood up. She remained face down on the bed.

He turned and banged into the door, allowing his forehead to smack into the wood. It swallowed the sound. He put his hands around his own neck and squeezed, until the blood throbbed in his temples and neck.

Scream.

The sound hummed in his throat, against his hands. He tried to contain it there. But it escaped.

He opened the door, slammed it behind him.

His foster mum had bought him an iced chocolate cake for his eighteenth birthday. He plunged his hands in wrist-deep, digging, scooping portions onto a paper plate, licking, wiping his fingers. What? he said, between mouthfuls. It's lovely. Nobody else touched any. He was half-drunk from his first visit to a pub, but he got through six pieces before he puked.

In Venice, he woke up with unexplained liabilities. His pyjama trousers lay in a sodden ball on the floor – but the mattress was dry and the pyjamas didn't smell of anything. His right temple was livid and swollen, as if he'd been struck there. Scabbed scratches on his left ankle, but no blood on the sheets. Instead, spots caked on the pillow. Scrapings, oozings.

When he'd washed and dressed, he brought the large-format camera through to the lounge. He set it up; broke it down; set it up again. He wanted to link the rhythm of the machine to the rhythm of his body. To think with his hands as well as his eyes. Or cease to think.

He released the locks on the tripod legs and extended the tubing. The locks were stiff. They required an exaggerated effort to open and close.

A headache, of course.

He snapped the collapsed camera body into place on the tripod head.

An internal beat.

He loosened the screws, and pulled the rear standard upright.

His blood carried the beat from his head out to the rest of his body.

He unfolded the camera bellows and aligned the front standard.

Dry, foul mouth.

He tightened the screws on the camera body.

He swallowed bile.

He attached the wide-angle lens and board to the front standard.

Sweat like unstable gelignite.

He cocked the shutter.

His cock shrivelled.

He set the lens to maximum aperture, and opened the shutter.

Skin coarse as a spent match head.

He focused the lens on the wall.

Face a desiccated mask.

He closed the shutter and stopped down the lens.

Eyeballs heavy with blood.

He inserted the darkslide at the back of the camera.

Nausea.

He removed the slide cover to expose the sheet of film inside the sealed camera.

Internal organs swollen.

He tripped the shutter. It whirred mechanically, for one-quarter of a second.

Gut gurgling.

He reinserted the slide cover and removed the darkslide from the camera back.

Bowels twitching.

When he worked outside, he checked the alignment on the tripod head from every angle before he took the exposure: two steps back, check; three steps forwards, check; one step left, check; two steps right, check. A cruciform pattern.

He was a fixed sequence of actions; he was a collection of symptoms. His hands shook; the tripod didn't. Amen.

UNNUMBERED LARGE-FORMAT NEGATIVE:
RIO TERÀ SANT'ANDREA, 17M

Arbus said: there's what you want people to know about you, and what you can't help people knowing. That's what a portrait's about. I say: there's the thing I want to photograph, and all the things I can't avoid photographing. I try to see everything in the frame – the grid on the viewfinder, square by square. But it's impossible. And that's *what the picture's about.*

This is a seventeen-minute exposure. The car on the right is there for the first eight. The driver changes a baby's nappy on the hood; he walks over, puts it in the rubbish bin on the left; returns to his car, drives away. All invisible, below the camera's threshold of attention.

About the same time the first car leaves, the Mercedes in the middle backs into the frame. The driver gets out and says, Am I spoiling your photograph? Anzi. You're doing something *to it, but you're definitely not spoiling it.*

All that's invisible too, and both cars are half there. By which I mean, they're each there for half the exposure. What the photograph doesn't register is their direction. Time's a vector, but it runs both ways. Meets in the middle, and bleeds out both ends.

A third car in the background. Not visible at all, only a parabolic slash through the gates, which open electronically for a minute, then hum shut.

All these things exist in the gap that opens up between the camera's attention and my perception. It's always there, that gap. What photography's for: to explore it, to articulate it as precisely as possible. The longer the exposure lasts, the wider it grows.

10

LARS'S GRADUATION PARTY. A ROLLING CELEBRATION. NO obscene posters, flour or eggs – but it took him five years to get the degree, so the occasion deserved more than a packet of Pringles at Enzo's. His shifting caravan of friends had already called at several watering holes in and around Santa Margherita. They got to the Postale about ten thirty: a small bar with French pretensions, the drinks menu written by hand on the wall in a flowery script. Its main advantage tonight was its location halfway to the Scalzi bridge back to Cannaregio.

Merlo had already graduated, back in July, but she'd stuck around so she could share this occasion with Lars. She'd been working at Bianco e Nero to pay her way for the last several months. But after tonight, everyone was leaving Venice: Merlo, Lars, Richard – only Lucia would remain.

The four of them stood outside the Postale with Guido, one of Lars's Italian friends, who was explaining how entertaining it was to sit in on Lars's dissertation defence, which was a public event.

At the end – Guido could hardly get the words out for laughing – this idiot says, 'Non me ne frega niente!' And the three old guys on the panel look at him like he farted.

I was trying to say, 'I don't mind,' Lars explained.

But it's more like, 'I don't give a shit,' Guido said.

It doesn't rub me? Richard said.

It used to be a fascist motto, Lucia said. I think that's one of the reasons it's rude.

So are you declaring yourself a fascist by saying it?

No, Guido said. It's just incivile. He nodded towards Richard's feet. But you know your shoes declare you to be a communist?

Richard regarded his ruined desert boots, which he kept insisting on bringing back to Venice. Why? he asked.

It's one of those tribal things. I got beaten up at school when I wore a pair without knowing what it meant.

'It doesn't rub me,' Merlo said. Surely the meaning is sexual?

Pervert, Guido said.

I blame Enzo, Lars said. I get all these sayings from him.

Richard would do well in exams, Lucia said. He sounds very polite in Italian.

Because I learned from reading academic books, Richard said. He turned to Lars: Now I live round the corner from Enzo's, I see him out and about. He was on the Rio Terà yesterday with his little girl. She was riding a tricycle round him. The only time I've seen him laughing.

He doesn't live in the serving hatch you know, Lars said. He's not a troll.

But it's always a surprise, seeing people outside the context you know them in.

Do you think guests from the hotel where you worked were surprised when they saw you outside? Merlo asked.

You're right. It shouldn't be a surprise.

I know what you mean, she said. We assume everyone else lives for their job: they're *delighted* to serve us. But when we're working, we can't wait to get home.

Bianco e Nero is okay though?

Developing other people's negatives isn't as much fun as you think.

There must be some good photographers. Me, for example.

I've actually done a couple of your Delta 3200s. They take forever. But Vito won't let me touch large-format.

Guido put Lars in a headlock, then rubbed his exposed crown with the knuckles of a clenched fist. Non me ne frega niente! Non me ne frega niente!

Yes, yes, very amusing, Lars said, but if you could let me go now.

Vieni dentro e parla con noi, Guido said, now playing Lars's scalp like a bongo drum with his free hand.

I will if you let me go.

Lucia and Guido accompanied Lars inside.

Merlo had borrowed Lars's duffel coat for the evening, and she was wearing it open but with the hood up. Beads of water from an earlier shower glistened on the rough surface of the wool. She had her Pentax slung over her shoulder inside the coat. Underneath that, she was wearing a charcoal-coloured wool dress. She'd also had her hair done. She looked like a present, half-unwrapped.

Do you want to sit down? Richard asked. There were iron railings along the side of the canal here, so there were also a few two-person tables from the Postale strung out inside them.

It's wet.

Richard unwound the rangefinder strap from his left wrist and pushed the camera into his coat pocket: with the 35mm lens, it was just about flat enough to fit. Then he pulled one of the tubular metal chairs back from its table and brushed the seat. Cold droplets scattered under his hand. Maybe you're right, he said. He straightened up and watched his breath form and disappear. He fastened the top button on his leather coat. Aren't you cold? he asked. Why are we outside anyway?

Because it's too hot and crowded in there.

I'm going to miss you all, he said, looking out over the canal.

We're going to miss you too.

I'm going to miss *you*.

Merlo linked her arm with his and lay her head on his shoulder. Neither of them spoke for a minute.

I wouldn't have started taking photographs without you, he said.

So you have me to thank for dropping out of Cambridge.

It was worth it. I'd do it again.

But I've changed too, from watching you. You think about everything. And I can see you thinking, with your body.

I didn't know you could do that, before.

She pulled away from him. I need to say goodbye to a few people, she said. Will you wait for me out here?

Yes.

She pulled her camera out and moved back inside the bar.

Richard looked up. The air had that special clarity you only got after rain, the stars hard and bright. On a large-format negative, they showed up like flaws, like specks of dust.

Lars came stomping through the door of the Postale, holding a pint glass in each hand. I brought you a beer. What are you doing?

Looking at the stars.

Lars put the glasses down on one of the outside tables and followed Richard's gaze. Yep, they're still there.

Not all of them. Some of them have already gone – the news just hasn't reached us yet. Richard picked the pint glass up. Thanks.

You have to come and visit me in Denmark.

Do you have to go back?

My stepdad won't keep paying. And there's a family flat I can use in my hometown.

That's good.

It's scary, though. When you say, 'I'm a student,' no one expects anything. You're still learning. But now I have to say, 'I'm an artist,' and suddenly everyone's got an opinion about what that means, and how I'm not living up to it.

What's happening with Lucia?

Ah shit man. I was having a good time.

Sorry.

Lars extracted a cigarette from a packet and lit it. Richard had always envied smokers for this ability to punctuate their conversations with dramatic pauses.

I don't know what's happening, Lars finally said.

She has to stay here?

Of course. And even after she graduates, there's not much work for Italian–English translation in Denmark. I guess we'll find out whether long-distance relationships are possible. But what's happening with you and Merlo?

Me and Merlo? I don't think there is a 'me and Merlo'.

You like her, though, right?

Richard shifted his weight from one foot to the other. Yes, he said.

So what have you got to lose? We're all gone in a few days.

Because I'm not sure what she thinks. And in my – admittedly limited – experience, if you're not sure, that means the answer's no. And if you insist on pushing it anyway, that doesn't make you romantic. It makes you an arsehole.

She's hard to read, like she's playing poker all the time. And in the years I've known her, she's never had a boyfriend – never even had anyone staying the night. But I've seen the way she looks at you.

She has had boyfriends though?

Yeesss.

Girlfriends then.

I suppose there's not much evidence either way.

Merlo and Lucia came through the door from the bar. What are you two talking about? Lucia said.

The stars, Richard said, glancing up again.

Lars flicked some ash off his cigarette and moved the glowing tip through the air in front of the two women.

Are you ready to go? Merlo said to Richard.

Give me a minute, he replied, and took several gulps from his beer.

Don't worry, Lars said. I'll finish it for you.

Ciao a tutti, Merlo said. She hugged Lars and Lucia in turn. Richard followed her example. Ci incontriamo tutti insieme per pranzo domani? Merlo said to Lucia.

Certo.

Ti chiamo nella mattina.

As Richard and Merlo walked away, he said, The Greeks believed the eyes emitted light. So perception happens outside the body, at the point where the light from my eyes meets the light from yours.

Eyes touching.

Yes.

As Richard and Merlo walked, their two sets of steps echoed each other, then separated. Too fast, she said. My legs are shorter than yours. Slow down.

Sorry.

Are you in a hurry to get somewhere?

It's habit.

She linked her arm through his again. This way I'll drag you, she said, like an anchor.

Anchors are useful, if you're in a storm.

A solitary bag seller on the Lista di Spagna tried to get Merlo's attention – they always zoned in on women – but she waved her hand. Mi dispiace. Then said to Richard, Funny. They don't normally bother me.

Maybe it's because you're in a dress and make-up.

It does increase the number of creeps, but there's no avoiding them, no matter how hard you try.

It was a special occasion tonight.

I wanted you to *see* me.

I always see you.

You never photograph me.

I don't photograph people I know, Richard said.

You did tonight.

Because I'm leaving. He looked at her. Do you want to go straight home?

Can we go to your flat?

Yes.

When they got to Sant'Alvise, he went first up the staircase to the front door. Why have I never been here before? Merlo asked, holding on to the hem of his coat with her fingers like she was blind and she didn't want to lose him.

I never invite people round. Not here, not anywhere.

Why?

Because nowhere feels like home.

But Venice does.

The flat does too, now. You coming here makes it home.

He finally managed to slot the key in the lock and the door clicked open. Hang on a second, he said. I want to check there's nothing shameful.

Like what?

Oh, you'd be surprised.

He left her outside but with the door open a crack. In the bedroom, he bundled his scorched, holey pyjamas into the chest of drawers. In the kitchen he stuck several empty bottles under the sink. Then returned to the front door.

Is this your bathroom? Merlo said, moving past him.

Yes, but be aware you're on stage if you turn the main light on.

Well, if anyone's been waiting out there to watch me pee, it's their lucky night.

Richard went through to the kitchen and ran the cold tap to get a glass of water, which he swallowed greedily, before pouring a generous splash of whisky into the same glass from the bottle on the kitchen table.

When Merlo came through he took her place in the bathroom – left the light on, following her example, but sat down so she wouldn't be able to hear him pee. He thought about taking a tablet, but decided against it.

Do you want something to drink, he said when he returned to the kitchen. Water, camomile tea? I've got some Coke in the fridge.

Can I have whisky in the Coke?

This really is a special occasion.

Is that blasphemy? Whisky and Coke.

It's only a shitty blend, not a single malt. Richard didn't drink single malts any more – it wasn't worth it, given how quickly he went through a bottle.

Merlo shrugged the duffel coat off her shoulders and disentangled herself from the Pentax, which she placed on the table.

I'll take your coat, Richard said, but he didn't have anywhere to put it, so he hung it on the back of one of the kitchen chairs.

Merlo took a step forwards and moved close to press herself against him. She put her arms around his neck and swayed from side to side, like she was dancing.

Do you want me to put some music on? Richard asked. He placed his arms loosely around her waist, and his hand hovered an inch above the small of her back.

In a moment, Merlo said. She leaned her weight against him, like she was about to faint and she needed him to keep her upright.

He took tighter hold of her waist. How drunk are you, exactly?

Exactly as drunk as I need to be.

So you'll still respect me in the morning?

Yes. How drunk are *you*?

Oh, you know, the usual.

You drink too much.

You're right.

But I'm not going to lecture you. She picked up her glass from the table and took a mouthful of whisky and Coke. She came closer again and pressed her cheek against his chest. She said, I want to stay here tonight. Can I do that?

Yes.

Why is it me who has to say this?

Let's go through to the lounge.

He led her by the hand into the next room and placed her on the sofa. Her eyes followed him as he put a CD in the player: *Stories from the City, Stories from the Sea* by PJ Harvey, which they'd all listened to constantly during the last three months in Venice. The first song was 'Big Exit': Merlo played air guitar along to the riff for a few seconds. Then she stopped and leaned back against the sofa. I don't do this, she said. I mean, not often.

Nor do I, he said. He sat down next to her. I like your hair like this. He brushed it behind her ear.

She took his glasses off. Who touches you? she asked.

I don't know. The barber.

Can I touch you?

She was the best kisser he'd ever met, or the best he could remember. He'd forgotten the others. Couldn't even remember this. As it was happening, he was forgetting. Trying to hold on, but he couldn't. She was a breath, escaping from his mouth.

He took Merlo's bottom lip between his, gently, and pulled away. The raised centre of his lips to the outer corner of hers. He relaxed his mouth: passive, receptive. She relaxed her mouth: passive, receptive. He moved forwards; she moved forwards. He stopped; she stopped.

Wait, he said.

I'm waiting.

He forgot himself, then remembered. Never wide open; never closed. Never zero; never one. The ego blinking on and off. He made a soft humming sound in his throat. Every sound was a movement, and he could feel this one pass from his mouth to hers and back again.

Hold her head. His hands were an extension of his mouth. He kissed her with his whole body; he held his whole body back. He kept the pressure generalised, his mouth slack, until the last possible moment, the moment before it became unbearable – before it was too late. And then it was too late – but it didn't matter.

The corners of her expression twitched. A smile or a frown? He drew back. A smile.

She leaned forwards, undid the top two buttons on his shirt.

I can do that, he said.

She stood up and moved in front of him. He put her arms around his neck and continued undoing his shirt buttons. When it was open, he touched the hem of her dress between his finger and thumb. How does this work?

It's pretty simple, she said, raising her arms in the air.

He stood back up, pulling her dress up as he did so.

There you go, she said.

He stepped up off the floor onto the sofa so he could get the dress all the way up over the pointing blades of her hands.

Abracadabra, he said, sitting down again. Rabbits out of hats.

She placed her hands over her breasts, even though she still had her bra on. Now I'm shy, she said. Her face was red, though that might have been the alcohol. Why am I shy?

You're beautiful, he said, pressing his ear against her stomach, as if listening for a foetal heartbeat. I can't see you anyway.

She ran her hands through his hair. I don't want to have sex. Is that okay?

You tell me what you want then.

Where's the bedroom? Let's go there.

He stood up and took her hand, led her past the kitchen and the gas heater. He turned up the setting and it whumped back on.

The bedroom was colder than the rest of the flat and the bed seemed enormous to him, with a walnut wood frame and headboard. No duvet, but a blanket, a quilt and a brocaded counterpane. He never made the bedclothes up in the morning, so they were mussed up on one side. He said, I confess I'm not entirely sure when I last changed the sheets. But definitely no longer than ten days. Anyway, the other side will be fine. Good as new.

Do you move over halfway through the month so you can keep them on longer?

He laughed. I change them more often than that.

She sat down on the bed and said, It feels dark in here.

This is where I load film, so I never open the shutters. You're lucky I don't have bin bags taped over the windows. But you don't need them, especially at night. He closed the bedroom door and turned off the light. See?

Can you open the door?

Sure.

There was a soft light from the courtyard coming through the bathroom window, spilling through the doorway and up onto the bed. Merlo slipped between the sheets and shuffled her body across to its undisturbed side. He got in beside her and lay on his back, arms at his sides, palms flat against the white sheet. She sat up and reached behind her to unclasp her bra.

That's a good idea, Richard said. You'd be waiting forever for me to get it undone.

There were no colours in the darkened room, so her flesh was grey against the inky shadows. She lay down again, and the covers rose as she lifted her knees and reached down to remove her knickers. She was still beside him for a minute and he listened to her breathe.

I want you to touch me now, she finally said.

Richard kept his gaze on the ceiling. Eventually he turned on his side. Can you say that again?

Touch me. She turned towards him. Are you cold?

No.

Why are you shivering?

I don't know.

Close your eyes.

Why?

We have to do everything blind. Like in the darkroom.

He closed his eyes and she moved closer, so he could feel her breath on his face. He placed his hand on her hip, moved it up her ribs and then down across her stomach. Moved in to kiss her again.

She shifted her leg and moved his hand between her thighs. Then placed her hand inside the elasticated waist of his boxers.

He wasn't himself. He wasn't her.

He was soaking. He was soluble in her.

He was expanding. He was a total sensation. He was hilarious.

Don't try to stop it; let it flow through you. Let the light flow through you.

He opened his eyes and the sound of her laughter filled the room.

Fuck, she said. Intense.

He thought he wouldn't sleep, but then he woke up and it was morning, and the other side of the bed was empty. He moved his hand across: cold. He wasn't surprised. But then he heard the moka caffettiera put-putting on the stove in the kitchen, and Merlo turning the gas down and pouring the coffee into cups.

She padded through on bare feet. Are you awake?

Yes. He pulled his head out from under the pillow, where he'd instinctively withdrawn when he thought she'd gone.

Can I open the shutters?

If you must.

She moved to the windows and he watched her – she was in her bra and knickers. When she lifted the bar holding the shutters closed, a shower of paint flakes fell on the sill.

Do you have milk and sugar?

Definitely milk. There might be sugar in one of the cupboards. What do you take?

With an espresso?

Yes.

A bit of each.

She went back to the kitchen, where he could hear her going through the cupboards and tutting, then tapping spoons, before she brought the espresso cups through and placed them on the bedside table. She'd also brought the Pentax with her, slung over her shoulder.

Seriously? he said.

Oh, but you look so nice.

Good job film doesn't register how breath smells.

She put her knees onto the rumpled counterpane, with her thighs and upper body upright, and shuffled up so she was straddling his stomach. She licked her fingers and smoothed down his hair, then pushed his head to one side on the pillow.

You know, with a wide-angle this close, it distorts the perspective. But you avoid that in profile. So stay like that.

Okay.

She was straddling his chest now and he was surrounded by her heat. The back of her left hand brushed his cheek and she moved the camera up to her eye with her right hand.

I feel like one of the models in *Blowup*, he said.

Stop talking.

NEGATIVE 276/30:
AL POSTALE, 1/30S

Over the shoulder, like in the movies. My elbows on the table, pushing all my weight down, leaning into the wood, using its resistance to steady the camera. To connect with the world.

Borrowing someone else's point of view. The look as a gesture – an action. The photograph as a gesture – an action.

My best drunk photograph. Maybe that's not relevant. It felt relevant, at the time.

11

THE QUEUES IN THE AIRPORT SNAKED AROUND AND DOUBLED
back on themselves. Richard had to take his shoes and belt off, and
throw his water bottle away.

In September, he'd told the college he was on a final research trip
to Venice, and he'd be returning in December. He didn't mention the
trip hadn't been approved by his supervisor – they'd find out soon
enough, when he didn't turn up for his evaluation. His fees were
paid up till the end of term, so he hoped they'd feel obliged to offer
him accommodation for a few weeks when he returned. He didn't
check his Cambridge email while he was away in case it contradicted
this assumption. He supposed he could always go back to Liverpool
if he had to – if he showed up on his foster mum's doorstep, she
wouldn't turn him away – and he was going to have to do that in
January anyway.

When he got in from Stansted, he wheeled his luggage from the
bus station to the porter's lodge; the suitcase kept bumping off its
wheels onto its side, so he was sweating by the time he got there,
even though it was a cold day. The porter checked his computer,
and stood silently for several minutes, reading something on the
screen. Yes, he finally said, there's a room for you – but I'm afraid
you have to be out before the new term. It says they've written to
explain why.

It's fine. I know why.

I'm sorry.

It's my own fault.

The official letters were in his pigeonhole: a blizzard of cross-referenced communications from the faculty, the college and the Scottish Office. An exasperated note from Professor Matlock and a more sympathetic one from Dr Christiansen as the chair of the assessment panel.

There was also a postcard from Dr Christiansen's friend in London, who ran the photography press. It had been six months since the seminar, and Richard had given up on him. His name was Roland, and he'd invited Richard to come and see him in a week's time.

Richard kept his finished prints wrapped in tissue inside the boxes the unexposed Ilford paper had originally come in – but he only had contact sheets from Bianco e Nero for the large-format negatives, because they were too big for the enlarger in the college darkroom. Should he prepare a smarter portfolio? What did that even involve? Maybe he should put everything in an album like Merlo did. In the end, he decided to take one of the Ilford boxes, and cut out some of the individual large-format images from the contact sheets. Because the negatives were so large, you could still make out the subjects even on a contact print.

The 'chat' with Roland was scheduled for three o'clock. The night before, Richard intended not to drink – took two tablets at nine o'clock – then ran to the off-licence five minutes before it closed. He woke up dull and heavy, but at least the hangover took his mind off things.

He took the train up to King's Cross early and went to the Photographers' Gallery near Leicester Square. They had a small exhibition with prints by Atget and others by Richard Wentworth, inviting comparisons between their work. Wentworth was a sculptor, but he'd been working on a photographic project around London for several years called *Making Do and Getting By*. Some of the images were of things Atget might have photographed: second-hand televisions piled in front of a shop, their individual prices rubbed with a finger through the dust on their screens. But others were quite different: a manky Wellington boot propping a door open, or a half-eaten bar of Cadbury's Fudge, still in its wrapper, stuck between an electric bell on a wall and its clapper, presumably to silence the sound, or polystyrene cups jammed between gutters and walls by people not quite willing to throw them on the floor, but also unwilling to wait until they reached a bin. It wasn't just that Atget used a large-format camera, while Wentworth seemed to have used 35mm; or that Atget's images were presented as brown albumen prints, and Wentworth's in colour. There were signs of individual agency in Atget's architectural pictures: a rug hung over a windowsill, abandoned carts in the street, a bicycle outside a shop. He made a point of *not* excluding these details – Old Paris might be historical, but it wasn't timeless. For Wentworth such details became the main subject, and the larger culture disappeared.

Roland's offices were in Bloomsbury, near the British Museum. Richard could probably have walked from Leicester Square, if he was more confident about London geography, but like most visitors his sense of the relations between places was entirely conditioned by the Tube map. Venice was the only place where he walked everywhere. He knew now: you needed to cross a space on foot before you could see it clearly. But he didn't need to see London. It was raining anyway.

The company offices occupied a converted Georgian townhouse, squashed between several others. He'd arrived early, but he didn't want to announce himself too far ahead of the scheduled time, so while he was waiting, he went for a macchiato at a nearby Italian café for good luck. He wanted to swallow a tablet, but somehow that felt like cheating in a way it hadn't for the paper in Cambridge. This was the meeting that was going to change his life, so he needed to be present for it.

The coffee was a mistake: his spoon betrayed him against the side of the cup. A maximum shutter speed of one five-hundredth of a second, with hands like these.

He rang the bell on the Georgian house at five to, and a posh male voice buzzed him in – told him to wait in the room to the left on the ground floor. A narrow, uneven staircase led up to the first floor, from where the posh voice was speaking to a quieter woman. Richard stood for a few seconds at the bottom of the stairs, but he didn't hear his own name or the word Venice.

The room on the left had a large, polished wooden table – an irregular shape, like a cartouche design – surrounded by plump chairs with bandy legs. One wall was made up of built-in bookshelves, to display the company's various publications. Richard went over to browse through them. There were also a few other books, reprints of classic monographs like *American Photographs* by Walker Evans and *The Ballad of Sexual Dependency* by Nan Goldin, presumably to invite comparison with Roland's photographers, whose names Richard didn't recognise, which made him feel stupid. The only contemporary photographer he knew was Merlo – and, after today, Richard Wentworth.

The posh voice continued its conversation upstairs – more like a monologue, the other speaker hmming occasionally, like when you were on the phone and you just needed to confirm to the person on the other end you were listening. At a quarter-past three, someone thumped down the stairs and swept into the room. Sorry, sorry, he said, holding out his hand in front of him like he was pointing a gun.

Richard stood up to meet him.

I'm Roland.

Richard.

Would you like something to drink? Tea, coffee, water? No espresso I'm afraid, but we have a French press.

No thanks, Richard said. I just had a coffee.

Roland took a seat on the opposite side of the table. He was middle-aged, but still thin, and his receding hair was cut short. He was wearing a rumpled suit. Richard didn't know much about designer labels, but he knew this was a Paul Smith from the five cuff buttons: someone had explained this to him once during a college feast. Roland also wore a V-neck jumper underneath the suit jacket. The building wasn't warm, or clean – the paint around the sash-window frames had seams of grime.

He said, Anna sent me a few JPEGs.

Richard touched the Ilford box on the table in front of him. I brought some prints.

How is Anna?

Richard wasn't sure how to answer this. Did Roland think he was friends with her? Okay, he said. I like her seminars. It was kind of her to write to you.

We were undergraduates together at Corpus, Roland said. More years ago than I like to remember. She said you've only been doing this for eighteen months.

Two years.

So why photography?

Richard blinked. The conversation suddenly felt like a job inter-view. He'd worn his pinstripe jacket and a formal shirt, but no tie; he didn't want to seem like he was trying too hard. The right choice: Roland wasn't wearing a tie either.

Richard said, The same reason I chose history. Because I don't want to make stuff up. I want to be accountable.

Roland pushed his chair back from the table and crossed one leg over the other. You use medium-format?

I borrowed an old Rolleiflex. But I switched to a four-by-five the last few months. I use 35mm too.

Okay, let's see what you've got.

Richard took the box of prints out from his rucksack. The older ones are toned, he said, but I'm afraid the large-format are only contact sheets.

Roland waved this objection away.

Richard put on a pair of white cotton gloves, like the ones the waiters wore at college, and pulled the lid off the box. He removed several prints – mainly on eight-by-ten paper, a few larger, the con-tact prints smaller. He unwrapped them from the tissue and started laying them out on the table in a row, facing Roland.

Roland stood up and removed a grubbier pair of white gloves from his left suit pocket. Once he'd put them on, he reached out his arm and opened and closed his left hand in Richard's direction. Just give me the box, he said.

Okay.

It's alright. I know what I'm doing.

Richard nudged the prints already on the table towards Roland, one by one, and then the box.

Roland lifted the box to move it so it was directly in front of him. Then scanned the unwrapped prints, which were now in a line above it. He moved the first one – which showed the Salute church in the fog with the gondolas – to the left of the box; also the second, of Rialto with the switched-off Christmas lights. But he placed the other prints on the table in a pile to his right. He didn't fold the tissue paper back over the emulsion before piling them. Then Roland went through the prints in the box, placing most of them to his right and a few to his left.

This all took about fifteen minutes, during which neither he nor Richard spoke. As the pile to Roland's right grew larger, Richard could feel it all slipping away from him – every possibility of a future. He wanted to stand up, sweep all the prints onto the floor and stamp on them, punch Roland in the face; walk outside; step in front of a bus. He tried to freeze his face into a death mask.

Eventually, Roland sat down again and leaned back in his chair, swinging one leg over the other again, and placing his gloved hands on his upper knee.

Two years is not a long time, he said. How old are you?

Twenty-eight.

Who's your favourite photographer?

I don't know. Walker Evans.

Yes, I can see that. Well, Evans started taking photographs in his mid-twenties, but I don't think he took a good one until 1929, and his best year was—

1936.

You'd know better than me. He was in his thirties anyway.

He had a solo show at MoMA in 1933.

And how old was he then?

Thirty?

Well, perhaps Walker Evans is not the most useful comparison. Do you buy many photography books?

I can't afford them. I look at them in the UL.

In fact. They're expensive to buy because they're expensive to make. So before I take something on, I have to *know* it's going to sell. Mostly that means an established name, but everybody I publish has a profile. Nobody introduces themselves to the world with a book.

Richard frowned. So, he said, if I go away and get a few exhibitions, and then come back—

I'm afraid not. There are some good photos here – Roland touched the small pile on his left – but a book isn't about a few good photos. It's about having a clearly defined subject – which has to be something of general interest – combined with a distinctive voice. I say 'voice': I mean eye of course. But it's easier to imagine a voice with a personality. In photography, the eye has a personality.

I went to see Richard Wentworth at the Photographer's Gallery.

And what is his subject?

Making Do and Getting By.

But that could mean anything. The decision about what to include under that definition is the voice. Because you go outside, and suddenly, everywhere you go, you keep seeing the things he photographs, which you've never noticed before. Or you've noticed them, but you haven't *looked*, because it never occurred to you they might be interesting, or they could be grouped together.

Atget photographed *all* of Old Paris.

And he took thirty years to do it. But even he organised his material. I published a book on manhole covers a few years ago. Hundreds of images, all identical. Except they're not. Putting them side by side forces you to pay attention to the differences, to see the variety. But it's the unity which allows that variety to become apparent.

Roland leaned forwards and placed his hands on either side of the box and the two piles of prints. He said, The fact that these are all of Venice does not in and of itself constitute a unity. This is like a lot of portfolios I see: all over the place. No voice.

It has lots of voices, Richard said.

Very good. But it won't do.

The subject is too big to describe with any one approach. Walker Evans did that too.

But a picture by Evans is instantly recognisable, Roland said. So what is your subject? And don't just say 'Venice'.

Richard thought for a moment, then said, It's not finished yet. It's a work in progress.

The photography?

Venice.

So what's the church with the gondolas doing here?

Well it's still there, isn't it? But so is everything else.

Do you know Luca Campigotto?

No.

You should. He did a book on the Arsenale; another on the old Stucky mill on the Giudecca. And one on hidden Venice, where he photographed at night. All large-format.

I don't like that. I like what's *not* hidden, what's staring you in the face. Richard fell silent. Was that even true? Yes and no. He would have liked to photograph the blank areas on the map – because those were staring you in the face too. He said, I couldn't get into the Arsenale.

I'm sure Campigotto spent a lot of time and effort figuring out how to get in.

He probably knows someone.

My point is he knows how to approach something systematically. He's also ten years older than you.

So I should wait ten years?

The difference between success and failure is often not giving up.

Well, thanks for your time. Richard was desperate to get out – before his entire world collapsed, before he screamed at Roland.

There are some good photos, Roland said. I'm glad I had the chance to see them. So please don't be discouraged. If this matters to you, it's worth persevering.

I don't have any money to go back to Venice.

So photograph somewhere else.

Fuck you, Richard thought. Perseverance. Where did the money for all this come from?

Outside, he walked a block away from the Georgian house, his feet splashing through the reflected Christmas lights on the wet pavement. When he thought he'd gone far enough, he stopped and raised his face to the sky. He made his hands into fists and finally allowed himself to scream. A woman approaching in front of him stopped abruptly, clutched her bags of Christmas shopping closer to her, and crossed the street. A man behind her kept coming, and gawped at Richard as he approached.

What the fuck are you looking at? Richard said.

The man swerved around him. Richard turned and watched his back as he walked away. He needed to swallow this anger, stop it rising up his throat. He walked into an off-licence and bought a half-pint of whisky.

He wished he'd stolen the copy of *American Photographs*. At least that way it wouldn't have been a wasted journey. Roland didn't understand. Richard loved orphan places. Because they accepted him; because he belonged there. And you could find these places anywhere, waiting to blossom with your attention – even Venice.

He should have said that twenty minutes ago.

NEGATIVE 282/8:
PIAZZA SAN MARCO, 8s

In a photograph, point of view isn't a metaphor. My eyes are five and a half feet off the ground, and when I look through the viewfinder, that's where the centre of the frame is: five and a half feet up in the air.

Change the parameters. Squat, lie on the floor, stand on a bench. Remove myself from the flow of traffic. Swap negotiation for contemplation. Acknowledge an object's power; make myself vulnerable. Look up. Only tourists do that. For Venetians, up doesn't exist.

A self-imposed rule, for the first 278 rolls of film. The camera only points into a space if I can imagine someone looking back at me, if I can imagine myself inside the frame, returning its gaze. So I can't look up.

A reliable way out of an impasse: do the opposite of whatever you did before.

The visual iconography of Piazza San Marco is so familiar, so inescapable. How much of it do I have to remove before the location becomes unrecognisable? No, that's negative. Put it in positive terms: how much of the context can I remove and still make it obvious where I am?

San Marco can be an orphan place too. The important space isn't under my feet, or in front of me. Not the interrupted space, rising up to block my path. Instead, the empty layer of air above my head, which is full of possibility.

I'm bankrupt: imaginatively, morally, photographically. On my knees, regarding emptiness. Who's looking back?

12

THE DAY AFTER HIS MEETING WITH ROLAND, RICHARD DIDN'T get up until noon. Then he lay in the bath for an hour and watched his fingertips prune; sat in his room staring out the window and put on the Sigur Rós CD with the drawing of an angel embryo on the cover. A good darkroom album: its pulsing swells sounded like they were filtered through uterine blood. Had Richard's mum always been dreaming of her escape? Was that what he'd absorbed from her?

At three o'clock, he went to call Merlo from the place near Market Square where you could make cheap international phone calls. It was always busy, so Richard had to wait a few minutes to get a free phone. A babel of different languages – most of the customers were obviously students, but perhaps some of them worked in hotels and bars.

Eventually the employee at the front desk pointed him towards an empty cubicle. Like all the others, it had a chair and a handset on a shelf. A laminated list of international dialling codes and minimum prices per minute for specific countries was stuck to the wall above the phone. Richard closed the door behind him and sat down. Holland was only a few pence a minute if you were calling a landline. Merlo was expecting his call, and she picked up quickly.

How did the meeting go? she said.

Richard threaded the spiral cord of the phone through his fingers, until his hand was tangled in its knots. Then he closed his fist and squeezed. Not well, he said.

What did he say, exactly?

He liked some of them, but I don't have an argument or a voice.

Well, I don't agree with him. But he wanted to meet you.

I think that had more to do with Anna – Dr Christiansen.

Do you think he asks to meet everyone?

Somebody's knee or elbow bumped the partition wall in the cubicle on Richard's right, and the man's voice rose as his speech got faster. I don't know, Richard said.

A publisher's never asked to meet me.

But you've had a gallery show.

At a shitty gallery. I won't bother again.

Why?

Because you get a decent turnout on the opening night, but after that ... I sold three prints – to my mother and her friends. So I paid her back for the gallery fee with her own money. Next time I'll put it on in the coffee shop.

How's that going?

Fine.

And you found a place to stay?

A girlfriend I knew from before I went to Venice.

Richard listened to the rise and fall of the conversations around him. On the other end of the line, he heard an ambulance siren pass Merlo's window.

It's fucked, he said.

What is?

You know, I only did a PhD because I didn't know what else to do. And I wanted to see how far I could go, where my limits were. Now I know.

Oh fuck off. It's only one rejection. I have a friend who's a writer – he's had dozens.

Richard said, In my final year as an undergrad, I saw what other people were applying for. The civil service: bullshit and overconfidence.

Management consultancy: as far as I can tell, the main function of that is, you come in, and you tell the bosses how many people they can fire. 'We'd like to keep you, but the consultancy guys say we can't.' And finance: that's a fantasy world. But it ruins real lives. I want to *make* something.

In Amsterdam, Merlo sipped something from a cup.

I'm going to have to go back to the fucking hotel, Richard said. I can't bear it.

The coffee shop's okay. I go home at night and leave it behind.

Yeah, the other problem with all those jobs, you have to convince them how much you want it. Nobody ever insisted I *enjoy* a night shift at the hotel.

Did you tell everyone there you were going to be a big shot?

No, but I let them say it. They'll be delighted to see me again. If they can't get out, why should anyone else?

Didn't you tell me your foster mum was proud of you?

And now she'll be ashamed.

Merlo tutted. If you hate the idea so much, don't go back.

Where else am I going to go? There's no money. I have to get a job.

Come here.

Richard listened to Merlo breathing down the line.

Amsterdam? he said.

What's stopping you?

Richard pressed the phone between his cheek and shoulder to free his hands and pressed both of his palms down against the shelf in the cubicle. I don't speak Dutch, he said.

You didn't speak Italian either. And if you're going to work in a hotel, you might be able to get a job here with English, Italian and just a little Dutch.

I want to print my negatives.

You can do that too – same place I do mine.

Do they have a large-format enlarger?

Yes.

Where would I stay?

With me.

Won't your flatmate mind?

Not if you pay rent, no.

In your room?

Yes.

In your bed?

Merlo laughed. Do I have to make my mind up right now?

No.

That's generous of you.

My point was – what would I be coming out there as? Your friend? Your boyfriend?

I don't know. But I want you to come.

Richard saw himself standing outside Merlo's apartment at some future date, looking up at the windows – like he stood outside Camille's house. Only in Amsterdam he'd have nowhere else to go. He said, There's something I never told you. Something that happened to me. Something I did.

What do you mean?

With another woman – *to* her.

How bad is this?

I don't think that's my place to say. But it's not good.

Why don't you tell me now, if you feel you have to?

The man in the next cubicle finished his call and left. When he pushed the door closed behind him, the glass in Richard's door rattled. The man on Richard's left started shouting down the phone in what sounded like Czech.

Not here, Richard said, pulling his chair forwards and hunching his body over the phone handset.

So tell me when you get here.

You might feel differently about me.

I suppose you'll have to take that risk. But if *I'm* willing to take it, you should be too.

I have to be out of here by the fifth of January.

That works for me, Merlo said. I'll be back from my mum's.

I'll check the flights and let you know.

Bring euros, not guilders. Holland's changing over on the first.

I told you. I don't have any money.

You'll get a job.

How much do you make at the coffee shop?

We'll manage. But if it takes you a while, maybe no printing. No drinking either. That might be harder for you.

Let me think, Richard said. Because it might be worse than that. Getting back to his doctor in Liverpool would be more complicated, so it could mean no tablets as well. But wasn't he sick of the endless hangovers, the grimy veil between himself and the world? Didn't he want to see things clearly – see Merlo?

There are no promises, she said. The only thing you're guaranteed: if you keep taking photographs, you'll get better. Do you want to get better?

Yes. I want to be better.

Then you'll get what you want.

The next day he received a package from Amsterdam in the post: a Kodak box that originally held unexposed colour paper. Inside, a handful of finished prints. They were all of Richard – or rather, he was in them all. The first was from Café Blue on the night he'd met

Merlo. She'd taken it when they'd all stood up to leave. It showed half of Lars on the left, next to Lucia, who was smiling back at the camera, and finally half of Richard, echoing Lars but at the right side of the composition. On the back of this, Merlo had written: *Already one of us.*

The next image was of Richard asleep on the couch in Merlo's apartment, his face dappled with sunlight coming through the slats of the blinds. Funny, because he didn't think he'd slept that night. What else had he got wrong?

The next photo was from Paradiso Perduto, Richard's camera held up to his eye, laughing into Merlo's flash. He wasn't used to seeing himself smile in photographs – or rather, he was used to the simpering grimaces people insisted you adopt when they asked you to pose and then made you hold the moment, which Merlo never did.

Another of him with Lars at the Postale, their arms around each other's shoulders, Lars leaning in to whisper something in Richard's ear. And the final one: his head turned to one side on the pillow of his bed in the apartment at Sant'Alvise, Merlo's arm coming into frame from where she was straddling his body, the back of her hand touching his cheek.

He looked happy. Not just in the last photo. In all of them.

On the day before he flew to Amsterdam, Richard went back to the college darkroom to work on a negative he hadn't printed before. Taken on a wretched day from a vaporetto on the Grand Canal. He was pointing the camera out, pretending to frame the scenery, which had presented itself only through translucent sheets of drizzle, but he'd focused on a fogged navigation mirror, high up at the side of the pilot's cabin. In the mirror, he was visible, holding the rangefinder, which was pointed towards Merlo, who was also doubled in the foreground, filling the frame, unrecognisably distorted by the open aperture. He was photographing himself photographing her.

Merlo taught him: every photograph was a photograph of a relationship.

When he took this image, he set the exposure off the misty reflection in the navigation mirror, a pool of even deeper shade within an overcast scene, so in the print, the grey, wet background blew out. But it wasn't quite empty. Little flecks of palazzi showed through, even at the high contrast necessary to resolve the reflection in the condensation-soaked mirror.

When he exposed the print, he dodged the background. Usually you dodged to reveal additional information in the shadows, but here he was doing it to remove information from the highlights. He moved his fingers in and around Merlo's distorted silhouette, as if he was playing a theremin. His hands blinded the enlarger. He couldn't look at her directly, only her reflection. And he couldn't touch her either, only the space around her.

The darkroom wall above the tray was now entirely covered in postcards she'd sent him from Venice over the last two years. When he packed everything away, he left them up there. Postcards, like photographs, marked absences – but he was going to be present with Merlo in Amsterdam.

Imagine a future. A reliable way out of an impasse: do the opposite of whatever you did before.

On the morning of the day he flew out, Richard took his camera gear to the shop on King's Parade where he'd bought it and traded it all in for a Nikon D1X, a digital SLR with a zoom lens.

Light burns the emulsion. A stigma: a sign, a point, a branding mark; *plural, stigmata. So I don't penetrate; I'm penetrated. But light doesn't pierce my side, my hands, my feet. It pierces my eye. Which isn't a weapon. An open wound.*

The eye becomes an organ of touch, because it is itself touched, sensitised. It endures what it sees.

The wound in my eye is also a wound in the world. Reality bleeds onto the film. Photography's a double sensation, folded in on itself: seeing and being seen; touching and being touched.

Photography's not my medium. My medium's the body.

Part Two

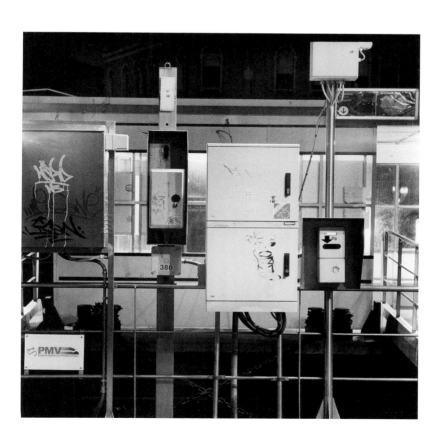

LIST OF IMAGES IN PART TWO

Vaporetto on the Grand Canal

Viewing platform on the Grand Canal

Rialto vaporetto stop

Prison and guard, Santa Maria Maggiore

Palazzo Ducale

Café, Piazza San Marco

Vaporetto in the Bacino di San Marco

Rialto

Temporary cinema in Piazza San Marco

Santa Maria del Giglio vaporetto stop

Piazza San Marco

Duckboards in Piazza San Marco

Ca' d'Oro vaporetto stop

Santa Maria dei Carmini

Dredged canal

Vaporetto on the Grand Canal

Sottoportego, Giudecca

Sottoportego, Piazza San Marco

Sottoportego, Castello

Vaporetto on the Grand Canal

Sottoportego, Cannaregio

Sottoportego, Sacca Fisola

Sottoportego, Giudecca

Bacini vaporetto stop

Public housing, Cannaregio

View from Tronchetto

Sant'Angelo vaporetto stop

Rio Terà Sant'Andrea

Rio Terà Sant'Andrea

San Zaccaria vaporetto stop

Ambulatory in the church of San Zaccaria

Bridge of Sighs

Rialto vaporetto stop

Santa Maria della Salute

Ponte della Paglia

Al Postale

Vaporetto on the Grand Canal

Casanova nightclub, Strada Nova

Café, Piazza San Marco

Tronchetto

Piazzale Roma

Vaporetto route map

Lido

Lido

Motonave and disused vaporetto stop

Venetian lagoon

Lido

San Tomà vaporetto stop

NOTES

All photographs are by the author. For the most part, their file numbers, locations and the circumstances surrounding their creation are described accurately, but their relation to the events of the novel is fictionalised. I have also sometimes falsified the order in which photographs were taken for narrative convenience (particularly for the images interpolated within the narrative chapters). In reality, the Polaroids were taken in late 2000 and early 2001, except for the one in the first chapter, which was taken in September 2004; all the other photographs were taken between February 2002 and March 2005, except for three outliers from March 2008. The novel compresses this timescale into a shorter period from 2000–1. For a few images, I used additional lenses for both the 35mm rangefinder and the large-format camera besides those indicated in the novel; for two of the images from 2008, I also used another camera, a medium-format Mamiya C330 with a telephoto lens.

Some of the Polaroids included here appear in my first (non-fiction) book, *Pistols! Treason! Murder!: The Rise and Fall of a Master Spy*, from which I've also adapted a few lines of related text. The novel's coda paraphrases ideas from the phenomenology of Maurice Merleau-Ponty.

I wrote a very different version of this book when I was an MFA student at the University of Glasgow – I would like to thank my supervisor there, Zoe Strachan, for her feedback on that version. Kate and Nick Eckstein kept my negatives safe for a decade, and returned them to me in 2021. I'm grateful to Lachlan Young for his expertise in scanning many of the negatives and his advice on the selection and sequencing of the images in Part Two.

Thanks also to Martha Sprackland for her copy-editing, and to Irene Marcuccio for checking the references to Italian language and culture. Finally, I would like to thank my publisher Henry Rowley for taking on such an unusual book, and committing to the photographs.